'Oh no!'

The muted cry was wrenched from her. She couldn't go back into that room and face all those people again. A strong, lean hand, as brown as her own, closed over her clenched fist.

'Don't,' said Dr Devenish. 'You'll hurt yourself.'

Toni turned a ravaged face towards him. 'It doesn't matter,' she mumbled. 'This was all a mistake.'

Dear Reader

Caroline Anderson gives us the final part of her trilogy, KNAVE OF HEARTS, where Anne meets her Jake again after eight years—a tearjerker! OUT OF PRACTICE is Lynne Collins's fortieth book for the medical series, and it is a lovely story set in general practice. I know you will enjoy it. Margaret O'Neill's hero, Rupert, is touchingly protective of Toni, and, to round off, Sheila Danton takes us to India, with all that country's problems and joys. See you next month. . .

The Editor

Margaret O'Neill started scribbling at four and began nursing at twenty. She contracted TB, and, when recovered, did her British Tuberculosis Association nursing training before general training at the Royal Portsmouth Hospital. She married, had two children, and, with her late husband, she owned and managed several nursing homes. Now retired and living in Sussex, she still has many nursing contacts. Her husband would have been delighted to see her books in print.

Recent titles by the same author:

DOCTOR ON SKYE
IN SAFE HANDS

SEEDS OF LOVE

BY

MARGARET O'NEILL

MILLS & BOON LIMITED
ETON HOUSE   18–24 PARADISE ROAD
RICHMOND   SURREY   TW9 1SR

To my son Chris and daughter Jo—
thanks for everything

First published in Great Britain 1993
by Mills & Boon Limited

© Margaret O'Neill 1993

Australian copyright 1993
Philippine copyright 1993
This edition 1993

ISBN 0 263 77999 8

Set in 10 on 11pt Linotron Times
03-9302-57312

Typeset in Great Britain by Centracet, Cambridge
Made and printed in Great Britain

CHAPTER ONE

IF ONLY, she thought, her head jammed against the tractor as she peered at the diminishing water in the radiator, it were not so hot. She stood back from the vehicle and pushed the cotton cap from above her eyebrows, trailing a black smear of grease across her forehead.

'Oh, sh——' she said loudly, biting back the word that her late grandmother had hated. One of her very few prejudices. Toni smiled at the memory of that remarkable old lady with whom she had enjoyed a loving rapport over many years. 'I didn't say it,' she said, looking up at the brassy afternoon sky.

There was a rumble of thunder a very long way off. It vibrated and crackled round the horizon and rippled along the contours of the North Downs.

'Rain—please rain,' she muttered as she manoeuvred her head and shoulders under the tractor.

She heard a car swish along the drive and pull up a few yards away. Firm footsteps covered the space between the vehicles.

'Excuse me,' said a deep male voice, 'can you tell me where I might find Tony?'

Toni turned her head and examined the pair of well shod feet and trousered legs a few inches away from her nose. Nice voice, she thought.

'Won't be a minute,' she mumbled, and then said explosively, as a large drop of dirty water plopped into her eye, 'Oh, hell, it's leaking. You beast!' She thumped the underside of the radiator and more greasy water and a shower of dust fell on her.

'Anything I can do?' asked the voice, sweetly

reasonable. The trousered legs bent into a squatting position. A face appeared horizontally below the edge of the tractor, and a pair of eyes, blue as gentians, stared into hers.

'No, thanks, I'll see to it later,' Toni replied sharply, willing herself to respond to this friendly offer with cool reserve.

She scrambled out from beneath the vehicle and looked up at the visitor. He was standing high on the bank above her and his height was greatly exaggerated, a tall, broad-shouldered figure almost in silhouette against the strong yellow light of the sky.

A gust of strong wind whisked suddenly along the ground, lifting the leaves and drooping blossoms off bushes and a handful of dust from the oven-baked earth.

'I can't believe it,' Toni grumbled angrily through tight lips as some of the dust joined the dirty water in her right eye, making it sting and water painfully.

'Don't do that,' said the visitor, his voice sharp and firm with authority as she brushed her eye. 'Here, cover it with this.' He removed a neatly folded, snow-white handkerchief from the pocket of his linen jacket.

Toni did as she was bid, recognising that his instructions made sense even though she resented being commanded so forcefully.

She tried to ignore the hand that he offered to help her up the bank, but he grabbed her wrist and hauled.

'Now, let's go in there so I can take a look at that eye.' He pointed to the potting-shed on the other side of the drive.

'Look here,' said Toni, planting herself in front of him and finding that, even on the same level, she still had to tilt her head back to look him full in the face, with her one good eye. She could feel the other puffing up, and grit or something equally rough grating against lid and eyeball. 'You just stop ordering me about.

Thanks for the loan of the hanky, I've got one of my own here.' She fumbled in the pocket of her shorts.

'Yes, do put that over your eye and introduce a little more rubbish.' His voice was filled with irony. He raised one eyebrow in quizzical fashion, but the hint of a smile lifted the corners of his mouth.

'Oh,' Toni stuffed the crumpled tissue back into her pocket. Without further protest, and outwardly calm, she walked over to the potting-shed, but inside she was seething. She had had just about enough of men in general, and in particular today, with their blustering, bullying and their groping hands. She shrugged her shoulders as if this physical act could push away her unpleasant thoughts. Just try trusting someone and see what happens, she said to herself.

The thought made her pause again. She stopped at the door of the shed. 'Look,' she said, 'I don't think. . .' She couldn't finish the sentence. It was ridiculous to consider that this man would behave badly, however rotten some of his sex might be. He wouldn't give her any cause for alarm; everything about him radiated dependability, from the deep cultured voice to the unflinching blue eyes.

He finished her sentence. 'That you should trust me?' He looked down at her, examining her face carefully. 'Quite right to be cautious. I'm Dr Devenish—Rupert Devenish. I'm helping Dr Meredith out.' He held out a large but slim hand. 'And if you'll let me, I'll just check out that you haven't damaged that eye, then I'll be on my way to seek out this Tony whom the brigadier asked me to find.'

'I'm Toni—Antonia King.' She offered a small grubby hand. 'I'm sorry Grandfather sent you looking for me—he just doesn't realise that people haven't got time to go wandering around on his errands.'

'Good lord, it didn't register that Tony—Toni with

an "i", I presume—was a girl. The old boy—sorry,
the brigadier gave the impression. . .'

'That "Tony" was a rather superior and capable
orderly of sorts?'

'Well, yes, actually, though not in so many words.'

Toni managed a tight smile, a smile that widened
her already wide mouth and dimpled her cheeks, but
failed to reach her one visible grey eye, which
remained bleak and sad.

He said gently, 'Shall we sort out your eye problem
first and then discuss your grandfather's treatment?'

Toni nodded and stepped through the doorway into
the dimness of the potting-shed. It was a long narrow
building built against the cobbled wall of a barn, with
windows lining the north wall. It struck cool and
slightly damp after the fierce storm-laden heat outside.
A fan fixed to the roof after the style of some exotic
Middle Eastern hotel turned slowly and majestically,
moving the air gently from the open doorway through
which they had come to an exit at the top of a flight of
steps at the other end of the shed.

'How very refreshing and novel!' commented the
doctor, looking cautiously at the large moving blades
only an inch or so above his head. Assured that unless
he took to leaping about he was safe from the primitive
but effective piece of equipment, he indicated that
Toni should sit on a tall stool by the bench.

He stood behind her and removed the handkerchief
pad from her eye, now red and watering from the
irritation. 'Simple treatment first, I think. Pull your
top lid over the lower.' Toni obeyed. 'Ah, some
success.' He removed specks of dirt caught in her
lower lashes. 'Try again.'

She repeated the process, then he gently separated
her eyelids and asked her to roll her eyes in a complete
circle as he examined the cornea and pupil for further
debris or injury, with the aid of a pencil torch.

'Only superficial damage, but it will be a bit sore, I expect. You should wash it out a couple of times. I've some drops in the car; they should help.'

He fetched the drops, some gauze swabs and an eye-patch which he waved triumphantly.

'Found this in the first-aid box, not my case,' he explained. 'I remembered having to get it when we went to the beach a few weeks back and one of the kids got something in his eye.'

'Oh, really,' said Toni without enthusiasm. 'Do I need an eye-patch?'

'Stop you rubbing it for a while and prevent more dirt going in, especially while you're working. Head back.' He was standing behind her again, and she obediently tilted her head. Briefly her eyes stared up into the amazing blue of his, then his fingers were holding her lids apart as he instilled the soothing drops. He swabbed away a trickle of fluid that slid down her cheek.

His fingers were cool and sure in their movements, and Toni began to relax. 'We'll have to have this off,' he said, indicating her hat. 'To fix the patch.'

Toni pulled off her cap and a coil of elaborately plaited flaxen hair rolled down her back.

Dr Devenish stared. Fair hair he had suspected because of her long golden-brown eyelashes and pale smudges of brows, but not this magnificent rope of white-gold. He put out a hand to straighten the ends caught in the material of her shirt. His fingers touched her back, and she leapt off the stool and turned to face him.

'Don't do that—don't touch me!' she said savagely.

He looked at her face, pale with anger, and into her frightened, sad eyes.

'My dear——' He hesitated, about to say child, for she looked so young and vulnerable, but he was suddenly conscious that this might further offend, and substituted, 'Miss King, I was only releasing the caught ends of your hair.'

She stood facing him, her back to the bench, her breathing fast and shallow as she fought to control herself. Slowly her face regained some colour.

He held out the eye-patch. 'Would you rather fix this yourself?' he asked, his voice expressionless.

Toni stared at it and then at him and shook her head. 'No, you put it on, please. I'm sorry, I. . .' Her gesture eloquently described her earlier reaction. She reseated herself on the stool.

The doctor manoeuvred the patch into position.

'Do you want to put this on again?' he asked, offering her the cap.

Toni was grateful for his calm and unaffected manner. It was as if nothing had passed between them. She stuck the cap on her head in a straight, no-nonsense fashion, unaware that the peak jutting out over her smudged forehead and eye-patch gave her a jaunty, slightly raffish look.

Dr Devenish thought he might risk a comment. 'Very nautical,' he smiled, 'very *Pirates of Penzanceish.*'

For the first time in their brief acquaintance, Toni's face lit up completely and her visible eye lost its bleakness. 'Are you a Gilbert and Sullivan buff?' she asked.

'Well, not to say buff, but I enjoy most of their stuff. Legacy from my parents, I suppose—they were very keen.'

'So was Granny,' said Toni in a soft, affectionate voice. 'We used to sing together when we were working, updating the words to fit the day's news in the way that old W.S. would have done. It was such fun.'

Rupert Devenish, for some unaccountable reason and to his own astonishment, wished he could say something that would maintain her mood. Granny was obviously dead—the brigadier had mentioned 'My late lady wife'. It seemed that she had been greatly loved by him and his granddaughter.

He looked at this blonde-white young woman standing in front of him, and found himself for once bereft of words and consequently unsure of himself. This was such a novel experience that as he was casting around in his mind for a suitable comment he was also considering his own reactions.

It was fortunate that, as he had not reached a satisfactory conclusion about either matter, there was a tremendous crack of thunder from almost overhead and a great fork of lightning arced across the northern sky. Simultaneously the rain started.

Great globules of rain hit the roof of the shed, each with a single singing ping. Outside on the drive, the drops bounced against the hard surface, sending up showers of water. In seconds the drops merged into a waterfall of rain in such volume that the dry earth couldn't immediately absorb it. Runnels of water channelled their way down all the natural inclines.

'We'd better go through to the seed house,' said Toni. 'The water might come in here—bottom of the slope, you see.' She pushed a plastic bag of sharp potting sand over the doorstep and closed the door to the drive against it.

CHAPTER TWO

THE storm in fact proved a relief all round, Rupert thought later as he drove away. The rain had stopped, leaving the driveway, hedges and trees steaming gently in the sunshine. The sticky humidity preceding the storm had vanished and the air had lost the breathless quality that had made life uncomfortable.

A breathlessness, he thought wryly, not only caused by the sultry weather.

He had followed Toni up the steps to the seed house, fascinated by the swinging pendulum of plaited hair, glinting silver in the storm-filled light filtering through the windows. For a moment he had wanted more than anything in the world to reach out and touch it, feel the solid mass of hair constrained into the neat rope.

He was bowled over by the very idea of being tempted in such a manner. The sensation was both pleasant and faintly ridiculous, and not a little unnerving. His tastes, nicely controlled, ran to sophisticated women near enough his own age, not to—what was she?—nineteen or twenty-year-olds. Hell, at thirty-eight he could be her father.

He inhaled sharply, shocked at the wayward course his thoughts were taking.

Consciously he forced himself to take his eyes off the silver plait and found himself instead focusing on a neat pair of buttocks clothed in tattered blue denim shorts, on the steps in front of him, almost at eye level.

It must be the heat, he had thought, and loosened his tie. He was aware of breathing fast through an uncomfortably dry mouth as they entered the seed house. He cleared his throat.

Toni said, 'I should have warned you, the air in here is quite different, much drier, because of the extractor fans and lights and things.'

The seed house was unexpected after the cool, homely potting shed. There were hundreds of trays and containers lined up with military precision on shelves and benches. Some were beneath glass or plastic domes. Electric motors clicked on and off, regulating heat, light and moisture in automatic response to the needs of the seedlings and plants at different stages of growth.

'Granny called it our intensive care unit,' Toni said.

Rupert had been fascinated by her enthusiasm, the technical equipment and all the paraphernalia: the graded sections of seed trays, some showing only the merest fuzz of green, some containing inch-high seedlings. 'Waiting,' Toni explained, 'to be potted on.'

To a gardener of his limited interest and capabilities, the effort involved in plant production was a revelation.

He had time, as they toured the unit, built in an L-shape round the barn and much larger than the potting-shed, to gain control of his earlier riotous thoughts. He gave himself up to enjoying the company of this flaxen-haired and now animated young woman.

They finished their tour under the glass dome of a huge greenhouse, with slatted blinds controlled to open and close to admit just the right amount of light at any one time.

'What happens in the winter when it's almost dark all day?' Rupert asked.

'Well, the plants in here at that time usually need less light than these, but ordinary daylight is supplemented by artificial lighting just as it is in the seed house.'

'I didn't realise you were semi-commercial,' he said.

Toni gave a delightful giggle. 'I don't think Grandfather would appreciate semi!' she exclaimed.

Rupert looked blank, but only for a moment. 'Oh, of course—King's Seeds, rather more what one would call a going concern.' They grinned at each other, united by this small moment of humour.

They had stayed chatting in the greenhouse with the rain beating relentlessly on the glass roof and streaming down the windows. Thunder banged and rolled around the hills and great forks of lightning lit up the sky every few minutes.

Rupert encouraged Toni to talk, putting aside his reaction to her earlier with his usual self-control. This waif, he felt sure, needed to relax, to talk to someone, trust someone.

He learned that this part of the nursery was where King's Seeds had started some twenty-five years ago. The brigadier, now eighty-eight, had retired from the Army and moved back to his ancestral home, a delightful old Elizabethan manor house.

Granny had certainly been the prime mover in getting the nursery going—at first selling home-grown bedding plants and salad vegetables from the barn on a small domestic scale. She had used just three acres of ground between the barn and the manor house lawns. Timbers, the old house, was hidden behind a screen of tall trees, and the drive to it branched off the longer circular drive which ended in a sweep outside the barn.

To the south, a small hill known as the Rise separated the manor nursery from the thirty-odd acres given over entirely to commercial production. Over there were packing sheds and tunnel greenhouses and large tracts of land cultivated with shrubs and small trees for national distribution.

Nowadays, the original part of the nursery catered

mainly for the small shop at Timbers Garden Centre, which fronted the commercial operation on the other side of the hill. Toni, with some help, raised special house plants, herbs, and, in season, Christmas trees growing in neat rows up the side of the Rise.

'Do you specialise in anything?' Rupert asked, out of genuine interest but also to keep the conversation going and a happy gleam in her eye. The rain was easing, and he would soon have to bring the conversation round to the brigadier's treatment and take himself off.

Toni pushed herself from the bench on which she had been sitting and he leaning.

'Over here,' she said, leading him over to a wide gravelled bench filled with small bush roses. 'All these are special—miniature roses. Granny started work on them almost at the beginning of the nursery. She loved roses above all. It took about twelve years to produce the first variety and get them accredited, now we have three. This is Little Dolly Daydream.'

The name made Rupert smile; it was most apt for the little fat bushes and petite pink blooms. He sniffed at the flowers.

'That one hasn't much scent. It's quite hard, you know, to breed miniatures and retain or produce a perfume, but Granny did it with these two.' Toni pointed to a mass of bushes labelled Blood Royal and King's Coronet.

Rupert admired the small but vigorous-looking plants, the first with flowers bright as oxygenated blood, against dark glossy foliage. The scent was heavy, sweet. The other, though, was more to his liking. Tiny clusters of deepest red velvety blooms nestled against thick, pale green leaves, a reminder in miniature of the moss roses that bordered the lawns around his own home. A cloud of slightly sharp scent seemed to float around each small bush.

'A coronet indeed of blossoms and perfume,' he commented, bending to inhale the fragrance again.

Toni watched him, pleased with his response to Granny's specials. She'd been right to trust him, even though he was handsome and perhaps rather imperious, she thought, recalling the first few moments of their meeting.

The rain had stopped suddenly and the sun appeared blindingly bright. There was a whirring sound as the mechanism operating the blinds moved into action.

Just before the slats closed, the sun struck full on Rupert's thick brown hair, turning it copper-coloured.

'Oh!' Toni said, unable to keep the surprise out of her voice. 'You've almost got red hair.'

Rupert pulled a face. 'For my sins,' he said. 'It used to be blamed for any temper tantrums I threw as a child.'

'I can't imagine you. . .' Her voice petered out—after all, she hardly knew the man, it was rude in the extreme to make a personal comment.

'As a child,' said Rupert, his voice suddenly cold. Of course, she can't imagine me as anything but aged, he told himself.

'Why, no.' Her surprise was genuine. 'I was going to say that I couldn't imagine you in an uncontrollable rage, even as a child.'

'Is that by way of being a compliment?' He smiled in a way that made his long, clever face look whimsical.

'Well, yes,' she replied rather breathlessly, 'I—I suppose it is.' She blinked the one smoky grey eye that was visible and stared into his bright, almost violet pupils.

For a moment it was dim and very quiet in the glasshouse. Then they both became aware of small sounds—water running down the roof and gurgling into surface drains, the hiss of the automatic spray moisturising the plants, the metal framework of the glasshouse creaking as it responded to the sun's warmth, and, from outside, the birds trilling and chirping like mad now that the storm was over.

Rupert said foolishly, his voice husky, 'The rain has stopped.'

'Yes—yes, it has,' Toni agreed eagerly, as if he had made some prophetic and solemn statement.

'I'll have to be off soon.' He pushed back his cuff to expose his wristwatch, but didn't look at it immediately. 'I must sort out your grandfather's treatment.' His voice had been slow as if dragged from some great depth.

'Yes, we must,' automatically Toni had agreed. Still their eyes remained focused each on the other, Toni's one good one and his pair of brilliant blue, annihilating the space between them.

The telephone shrilled loudly. With a movement that looked as if it hurt, Toni turned herself round, pulling her eyes away from his, and marched zombie-like to the instrument that hung on the wall above the bench that was used as a desk.

She answered, 'Yes. No. In about half an hour,' and hung up the receiver. She stood for a moment gazing at the dead instrument, then jotted something down on a note-pad and turned slowly to face Rupert again.

While her back was turned he had put on spectacles. They were half-lenses, rimmed with a thin gold frame. They sat with comfortable familiarity on the high bridge of his nose, providing him with a sort of mask, through which he surveyed her.

She was busy trying to untangle her emotions. Had she imagined the breathless, silent exchange?

He was standing with his back to the south side of the greenhouse, and even though the brilliance of the sun was shuttered out he seemed to be in shadow with his back to the light.

She panicked for a moment—what had she done,

what had she revealed to this calm, large man? Had there been an exchange of wild, unspoken thoughts and revelations, a mutual exchange? Or had the messages, not even understood by herself, been all on her side? Had he simply been watching her, wondering if she was a dumb idiot of some sort? Was that why he had stared back?

'What about Grandfather's treatment?' she asked bluntly, not even daring to go on thinking about possibilities.

A flicker of unidentifiable emotion passed over his features. His eyes gleamed more brightly and his well marked lips tightened.

'Of course,' he said in a cool, expressionless voice, 'the brigadier's treatment. I think you'd better persuade him to let the practice nurse attend to the dressing on his leg ulcer.'

'Why?' If he could act indifferently, so could she.

'Because it's messy and really needs professional attention to assess progress.'

'And I'm not capable of doing that?'

Rupert looked at her carefully over the top of his reading glasses. How, he thought, do I explain that she, indeed anyone with common sense, is competent to do this damned dressing, but I—he repeated to himself in astonishment—I don't want her messing around with an unpleasant dressing on a bad-tempered old man.

Then he thought, what the hell, she's his granddaughter. She's a right to do it if she wants to, and she must have some sort of first-aid experience, the way the old boy spoke of her when I thought he meant an orderly or some such. She's probably done her St John's or Red Cross. It's not for me to stop her. Protect her, you mean, jeered his deepest inner voice. You want to take this silver-blonde creature, who looks like something out of an Arthurian legend, and lock her away somewhere, keep her for yourself.

Words from a book of love poems remembered from the innocent days of romantic youth popped into his mind.

> Deck her with flowers, jewels of the forest,
> Bind her with nosegays of love.
> Cord her with tokens of deepest devotion,
> Sing praises to heaven above.

Yes, he said to himself, that's precisely what I want to do—that and some rather more earthy demonstrations of love.

He blamed the heat and the strange light in the greenhouse for producing his dangerous and extraordinary thoughts.

Later he remembered thinking, God Almighty, I've flipped my lid. But a persistent voice inside his head assured him that he hadn't. He'd simply done what he had tried to avoid doing for years. He'd fallen, hook, line and sinker in love.

To Toni, standing watching him through her one grey eye, he said—and to her he sounded controlled, reasonable, 'No question of not being capable. Of course you are, only your grandfather's a rather forceful old gentleman and might be obstructive.'

'I've managed tougher propositions than Grandfather,' she assured him.

'Oh.' He hid a smile, amused at the way she drew herself up to her full height, all of five feet three inches, he guessed. Considering her eye-patch, swinging pigtail and nautical headgear, she managed to appear quite dignified. 'Well, there's nothing more to say, then.' He decided to give in gracefully.

He pulled a prescription pad from his pocket.

'I've written the brigadier up for a pack of special dressings and antiseptic lotion,' he said. 'Swab the

ulcer with the lotion and then apply the dressing daily
for the next three days. If there's an improvement by
then, leave the next dressing in place for two days. I
should think Dr Meredith will be visiting within that
time, but if you have any problems, please contact the
surgery.'

He had willed himself to sound very cool and
professional, but couldn't resist asking, on a humorous
note, 'May I ask where you learned your difficult-man
management?'

Quite what he thought her reply would be he had no
idea, but certainly her answer took him by surprise.

'On Men's Medical, Men's Surgical, Men's Ortho-
paedic, in Theatre, where most of the surgeons
thought they were God's gift to womankind, especially
the nursing staff.' Toni sounded angry and sarcastic,
bitter even.

Rupert thought he saw a glimmer of a reason for the
bleakness in her eyes and her shrinking away from his
accidental touch. She'd obviously had a bad experience
with some boorish medical man throwing his weight
about.

He was overwhelmed with compassion for this slender creature with the extraordinary hair, who in the
course of half an hour had exhibited toughness, gentle-
ness and, briefly, happiness.

What he was going to do about her and his feelings
long-term, he hadn't a clue. For the moment he must
leave her with a lifeline, with the feeling that she was
not alone—a tall order, based on an afternoon's
acquaintance, even allowing for the intimacy of the
eye contact earlier.

'So you're a nurse,' he said.

'That's right.'

'But all this——' He indicated the glasshouse and
the work sheds. 'Are you on holiday?' He didn't think,

from what she had said, that this was the case, but he felt compelled to ask.

'No.' She slid back the wide glass door leading on to the drive in a dismissive gesture. A wave of fresh-washed air greeted them.

Rupert tried again. 'Are you going to finish your training?'

She looked at him, her one good eye wide with surprise. 'I am trained—I took my finals nearly two years ago.'

He was astonished at the wave of relief that suffused him. So she wasn't nineteen, but at least twenty-three; she couldn't have qualified till she was twenty-one or thereabouts. He suppressed the huge grin that tugged at his lips. Fifteen years' difference in age was infinitely better than twenty.

'What a waste,' he said, 'of training and skill.' She looked shattered, bleak again, as when he had first seen her. 'Oh, I do beg your pardon—none of my business. There must be a good reason for what you're doing. My apologies.'

To be stricken twice in less than an hour with the inability to say the right words was alarming.

It was a nice apology, Toni thought, offered with cool sincerity.

'That's all right,' she muttered, feeling gauche and childish, wishing she could match his sophistication.

They walked across the steamy, glittering rain-soaked gravel towards his car. So much, thought Rupert, for giving her a lifeline.

'Shall I leave the prescription at the surgery for you to collect later? I understand that's the drill for country patients.'

'Please.'

'Will you be able to pick it up today? I'd like the brigadier to start his treatment immeidately.'

'Of course—stat.'

The hospital jargon sounded odd coming from this young woman in the middle of the country on a hot May afternoon.

Rupert wound down all the windows before folding himself into the small Fiat. The sun was dazzling after the dim greenhouse. It burnished the metalwork on the car.

Rupert ran long fingers through his thick hair and the sun gleamed on his ring and watch and cufflinks.

'Phew.' He gave Toni a lopsided grin. 'Still hot in spite of the rain, but fresher.' He proffered a hand, and once again she put her grubby paw into it. He cherished the moment. 'Goodbye,' he said, 'I hope all goes well with the treatment. Do phone if you have any problems.'

He put the car into gear and moved off slowly.

Toni raised a hand. He kept his eyes on her image in the driving mirror. A neat boyish figure, but with nice curves where it mattered, long bronzed legs and a patch over one eye.

She turned and marched back towards the greenhouse. The last Rupert saw clearly was the swinging silver pigtail hanging from beneath the cotton cap.

He accelerated down the drive. What you need, he told himself, is a very large whisky and half an hour with Brahms.

CHAPTER THREE

Toni stood in the driveway and watched the little car for a moment, then trudged back to the glasshouse. Her feelings about the doctor were mixed.

On the whole, she was sorry to see him go. He had been—she sought for the right words—reassuring. She coloured beneath her tan, remembering how she had chatted, and he had listened. Had she bored him by explaining about the plants and daily routine?

No, she decided, he had wanted to know and had been interested and surprised, like most amateurs, at the work involved. He had professed to enjoying pottering around the garden, doing the odd bit of mowing or weeding. 'Tidying up in the autumn,' he had said. 'Bonfires and things.'

As a GP, he must be very busy, and he had a family to look after. Children to take out on occasional treats, like visits to the seaside. Toni put up a hand and touched the eye-patch. Which of his children had needed it, she wondered, on their outing a few weeks back?

Why, she thought irritably, has Dr Rupert Devenish made such an impression on me? I've only just met the man! She set about loading the trailer attached to the Land Rover with the potted plants that had been ordered from the shop, and tried, unsuccessfully, to put the doctor out of her mind.

She thought about his wife and family, and, unwanted, came a picture of Mrs Rupert Devenish. 'I bet,' Toni said to the glasshouse at large, 'that she's one of those brainy, competent women, with a large family, and a career, and a husband to look after, and does it all supremely well.' For good measure, she added, 'And she's stunningly beautiful, and makes him blissfully happy.'

Perhaps, she thought wistfully, that was why I felt so comfortable with him, so unpressed, because he's obviously happy and contented with his lot. Everything about him is reassuring and solid.

She thought about the way he had looked that afternoon. His amazing blue eyes had mirrored various emotions, from twinkling encouragement when he'd pulled her up the bank, to cool appraisal when he'd considered her ability to cope with her grandfather's treatment. In fact, he had looked rather severe as he studied her over the top of his specs. She guessed he could be quite unyielding if those about him didn't come up to his standards. Would that apply to his children too? Was he a rigid disciplinarian expecting instant obedience?

Of course not. He would be the sort of father who would join in the fun; play games with his kids, encourage them to think for themselves. His casual comment about the beach party seemed to imply that, but there would be certain rules of behaviour, applied, and to be complied with, or evaded at risk of his displeasure. It was surprising how certain she was about her assessment of his character. Surprising, too, that she felt she had made a friend, a dependable friend.

How extraordinary, that after months of retiring into herself, avoiding people when possible, and opting out of social events, she should suddenly feel exhilarated, released.

That all this should have come about because of a brief encounter with the solid, handsome Dr Devenish was little short of a miracle. Perhaps the thunderstorm, and the lifting of the oppressive heat, had affected her. This was a nonsense, of course, and she knew it.

Better accept the fact that her visitor had been instrumental in rekindling her interest in life, and some sort of faith in humankind, and, specifically, mankind.

In the early evening Toni drove into Peckhurst to pick up her grandfather's medication.

It was just after six o'clock when she pulled into the Health Centre car park, and the May sun was still high and hot in the sky. The heavy rain had washed everything clean. Even the flowerbeds beneath the windows of the building, normally coated with dust, glistened with fresh life.

They look the way I feel, thought Toni, at least temporarily renewed. She smiled at the thought and jumped down from the Land Rover, unaware that she was being watched from one of the consulting-room windows.

Rupert Devenish drew in a sharp breath and parted the vertical slats of the blinds to give himself a better view. He had concealed, even from himself, the hope that she would come to the Centre while he was still on the premises.

'And here she is,' he muttered. 'What a cracker.' The old-fashioned expression seemed to suit her to perfection.

He moved along the window to keep her in view as she walked across the park to the entrance. She was wearing a daffodil-yellow shift dress that finished just above her knees. She had discarded her eye-patch. Her hair, unplaited, rippled in a silver stream down her back, beneath a wide-brimmed straw hat, which she wore flat, like a pancake, straight across her forehead. She walked, as she had walked from his car earlier that afternoon, with long easy strides in her soft-soled sandals.

'Wow!' was all the doctor could say as she disappeared from sight. He snapped the blinds back into position. He toyed with the idea of going through to the pharmacy area and accidentally intercepting her, but squashed it of necessity when his next patient arrived.

Toni marched into the dim coolness of the corridor and joined the queue at the 'presceiptions to collect' window.

Her friend Bridget Banks was on duty, and handed through the brigadier's package of medicine, as Toni, last in line, appeared.

'You've met him, then,' she said, rolling her eyes dramatically.

'Met him?' Toni put a query into her reply, though she knew very well whom Bridget meant.

'Our dishy Dr Devenish.'

'Oh, Dr Devenish—yes, he called to see Grandfather.'

'I know, I made up the scrip.' Bridget stared hard at her friend. 'Oh, come on, Toni, even you must have noticed him—those eyes.' She rolled her own again. 'And the thing is, he's so nice with it, with everyone. Doesn't throw his weight about, though, according to Dr Meredith, he's a real VIP in medical circles.'

'Is he here for keeps?' Toni asked, hoping she sounded just mildly interested.

'We should be so lucky,' replied Bridget. 'As far as I know, he's just passing through. He's a lecturer in GP studies at Princes. I think he's just looking us over. Anyway, there's a staff meeting tomorrow night, I might find out more then.'

Their conversation was brought to an end by the surge of people arriving to collect prescriptions.

'I'll give you a ring after the meeting if there's anything interesting about You Know Who!' Bridget called to Toni as she retreated to the doorway.

Toni waved a hand and removed herself as quickly

as possible, conscious of the interested glances from the waiting patients.

She was observed by Dr Devenish as she emerged into the evening sunshine. He had seen his last patient and again considered engineering a 'chance' meeting. Fate, Cupid, the gods, were not on his side, he decided, as there was a knock at the door.

'Come,' he called tersely.

To his surprise, Morris Meredith, the senior partner and his father's old friend, entered. Rupert had opened the vertical blinds to their fullest extent, so that he could view the car park, and Toni, clearly. He made to close the blinds, but Dr Meredith crossed to the window surprisingly fast, and, without being rude, Rupert found it impossible to close the blinds.

'Ah,' said the older doctor, homing in at once on Toni as she made to climb into the Land Rover. 'Little Toni—well, well, well!'

Reuprt realised there was no point in pretending he had not been observing her. 'Yes.' If he sounded curt, he couldn't help it; there was no evading the sharp eyes and instincts of his mature colleague, but he didn't want a discussion to develop.

They had both turned their backs to the window when there was a sudden burst of noise from outside. Metal on metal, as if chalk were being drawn screeching across a board, and a crunch as two heavy objects collided. Within seconds, over and above these sounds, came the scream of a woman's voice.

Rupert wrenched aside the blinds. Briefly both doctors stared at the scene in the car park. A small, nondescript van, with battered bodywork, was jammed against the rear of Toni's Land Rover, and a woman was struggling to open the driver's door, wedged against the larger vehicle's chassis. Even at this distance, and so briefly, Rupert could see that the woman was distressed, with tears streaming down her cheeks. She was shouting incoherently.

Rupert grabbed his surgical case and bounded for the door, with Morris Meredith a foot behind him.

When Rupert raced out into the car park he found a number of people grouped around and looking shocked. Toni was standing by the battered van holding a small child in her arms and pouring something from a bottle over the recumbent form. He reached her in a few long strides.

'Scalded,' she said in a tight voice. 'Arm, shoulder and chest. I had a bottle of water with me, I'm trying to cool the burn area.'

'Good. Is he in shock?'

Toni nodded. 'Semi-conscious, cyanosed round the lips, breathing laboured, but adequate.'

'Here—I'll take him, you take my case.' Rupert took the child gently from her arms. 'Let's get him inside.' He moved away with his almost motionless bundle, tilted slightly so that the head was lowered. Dr Meredith arrived. 'Morris, the mother.' He jerked his head towards the woman, who was still crying in a noisy, desperate manner.

Toni and Rupert hurried across to reception, where someone was holding the door wide. They went straight into the clinic-room. Without a word, Toni whipped away the pillows on the examination couch, elevated the foot and spread paper towels over the plastic-covered mattress. As soon as the boy had been laid down she covered the unaffected part of his body with a blanket.

Rupert gave her a brief, tight smile. 'Thanks. Can you help me cut these things away? There's no nurse on this evening.' Toni handed him scissors from the laid-up trolley and nodded.

'Do you want swabs and sterile water to soak off the material?' she asked.

'Please, and will you ask someone to phone St Botolph's for an ambulance? This child will have to be admitted.'

Dr Meredith came in at that moment, escorting the boy's mother. She had stopped crying and was obviously making an effort to be calm.

The receptionist on duty, new to Toni, responded at once to her request for an ambulance, and was already speaking to someone as Toni returned to the clinic-room.

The two doctors were bent over the child. His scalded arm was immersed in a bowl of water and Dr Meredith was swabbing the chest and shoulder of the small patient with sterile water. Part of the boy's T-shirt was adhesed to the burnt area on his chest.

'We'll have to leave that for the moment,' muttered Dr Devenish. He raised his head as Toni entered.

'All fixed?' he asked.

'Yes. What else can I do?'

'Reassure Mrs. . .?' He managed a smile for the distressed mother.

'White,' she said faintly. 'Doctor, will Simon be all right? He's not going to. . .?'

'You got him here very quickly, Mrs White, and that helps, and he's responding to the limited treatment that we can give. He's already less shocked than he was. Ask Nurse.' He flashed Toni a smile. 'She'll tell you how important this is, and I'm just going to give him an injection to ease the pain, to make his journey to hospital a little more comfortable.'

'Come and sit down, Mrs White. Will you have a cup of tea if I can rustle one up?'

Mrs White allowed herself to be led across the room and settled in a chair. 'He won't be disfigured, Nurse, will he?' she asked in a whisper.

For a moment Toni was at a loss how to answer. There was as yet no knowing how severely the scald might have damaged the tissues. The boy's hand and arm hadn't seemed too badly hurt, extensively affected but superficial, she judged, but his chest—that looked like a deeper wound.

'We won't really know for a while,' she said cautiously. 'But small children heal well. I think you'll be surprised how quickly Simon responds to treatment.'

There was a knock at the door and Bridget Banks walked in. 'Can I do anything?' she asked Toni softly.

'Tea, perhaps.'

'Sure, on the double.' Bridget retreated after giving Mrs White a reassuring smile.

Mrs White managed a weak smile in return. 'Everyone's so nice here,' she whispered to Toni. 'Not like they are in London.'

'Have you just moved down here?'

The woman nodded. 'I've left his dad,' she said, gesturing towards the couch and her son. 'He's rotten. I've got a job at the school up the road, cleaning and helping in the kitchen.'

'Where do you live?'

'On the caravan site, behind the the Red Fox. It's not bad,' Mrs White said defensively, seeing Toni disguise a look of dismay. 'He's all right, the chap who runs the pub, he lets us go in and have baths sometimes, and there's a shower in the caravan. We're not dirty,' she added belligerently.

'No, of course you're not,' said Toni gently. 'I was just surprised, that's all, when you said you were living there. I thought the caravans were only let out for holidays.'

Bridget came in with a tray and several mugs of tea. She put one into Mrs White's still shaking hands. 'Here, have a sip of that,' she said in a firm but kind voice. 'You know, the cup that cheers always makes you feel better.'

'You sound just like my mum used to,' said Mrs

White in a quavery voice, tears threatening again. 'She died last year. None of this would have happened if she was still here. Simon and I could always have had a home with her.'

'Can someone come and give us a hand?' asked Dr Meredith.

'I'll stay here,' said Bridget to Toni. 'You'll be more use there.'

For a moment Toni almost panicked. Although she had acted spontaneously in the emergency in the car park, she suddenly felt inadequate in this clinical situation, after a year away from nursing. Common sense told her that this was ridiculous.

'What can I do?' she asked in a cool professional voice as she reached the couch.

'Oh, Toni, it's you—good,' Dr Meredith said, sounding rather surprised. 'Look, can you find the chlorhexidine and lignocaine cream, I think it's kept in the cupboard over there, and a tulle gras dressing four by four, and zinc oxide plaster to fix with?'

Everything in the cupboard was plainly marked and neatly stacked. She found the items required within seconds; she cleaned her hands quickly with Savlon, slipped on a pair of plastic gloves, and was ready to open the sterile packs as soon as the doctors needed them.

They had managed, with sterile water and forceps, to remove the dirty material of the stuck T-shirt from the badly damaged area on the boy's chest. Dr Devenish applied the antiseptic cream that Toni proffered when she was sure he was ready for it, and Dr Meredith covered the site with the tulle gras dressing and held it in situ. Toni admired Rupert's long slim fingers at work on the small chest of the child as he carefully secured the dressing with zinc oxide plaster.

'Will you want a crêpe bandage or tubiform to cover?' she asked.

'A bandage, I think, don't you, Morris?' suggested the younger doctor.

'Yes, and clean gauze and coverings for the other injuries, Toni, if you can rustle them up.'

Like everything else in the clinic-room, and any other dressing-room attached to any well run hospital, she found that everything was to hand and clearly marked.

They had just finished working on the boy when they heard the ambulance arriving. Toni went to have a word with Mrs White, but it was Bridget who answered for her; she seemed to have established a strong rapport with the lady in the short time that they had spent together.

'Jenny's going in the ambulance with Simon,' she explained, 'and I'm going over to her caravan to collect some night things to take to the hospital and let Jim Cooper at the pub know what's happened.'

'What about Terry, won't he wonder where you are?' Toni asked Bridget.

Bridget dismissed her husband with a casual wave. 'Oh, he won't mind,' she said airily. 'He's playing cricket till light stops play, and then guess where I'll find him?'

'The Red Fox!'

'Exactly. I can kill two birds with one stone when I go to pick up Jenny's and Simon's things, see Jim, and leave a message for Terry if I don't see him.' Bridget whispered in Toni's ear, 'The poor girl hasn't got anybody to turn to. She and the kid are on their own.'

Toni nodded. 'That's what I thought. You know, she's only about our age too.'

'Yep, some people do have a load of bad luck, don't they?'

Toni nodded, and joined the little column of people following the ambulance men and stretcher out of the building. She stood with Dr Meredith, Dr Devenish, and the receptionist, who had remained, though surgery was long finished, to see the patient and his mother installed in the ambulance and leave the car park. They were followed by Bridget, who gave them a cheery wave. A few of the last patients for evening surgery had stayed behind in little animated groups. They dispersed with the departure of the ambulance, calling their goodnights as they left.

Rupert Devenish laid a detaining hand on Toni's arm as she made to move towards the Land Rover. 'Is your vehicle damaged?' he asked.

'Lord, I hadn't thought about it, but I shouldn't think so. The van's not much cop and smaller than the Land Rover; it's more likely that something's wrong with that.'

'Shall we have a look at it? The van will have to be moved before you can back out.'

His hand was still on her arm, and the thought came to her that she would have objected to the touch of any man whom she didn't know well prior to meeting him that afternoon. She was still quite bowled over by the impact that he'd made on her, and the extraordinary feeling of reliability that he exuded.

'Thank you, that would be kind.' She smiled, and he smiled back as they walked together to where her vehicle and the van stood jammed together.

In her distressed state Mrs White had run the side of her van into the bumper of the Land Rover and scraped along it, wedging the two vehicles together as she struggled to open the driver's door. The door was still narrowly open, and the keys in the dashboard, but they were inaccessible because the side of the van was almost flush with the Land Rover.

'I'll have to get in through the passenger door,' said Rupert. He tried closing the driver's door from inside before starting the engine, but something had gone wrong with the hinges and he couldn't budge the thing.

Carefully he eased forward with the door scraping along the bumper, but at last it was free. 'Sorry about that,' he said, easing his tall, broad frame out of the van via the passenger side with some difficulty. 'The driver's door won't budge, I'm afraid.' He bent to inspect what damage might have been caused to the bumper of the Land Rover.

'It doesn't matter in the least,' replied Toni cheerfully. 'It gets a lot of battering at the nursery. But what about Mrs White's van? I wonder if that's repairable. I bet she depends on it for getting everywhere.'

'Well, the steering's a bit dodgy, that's for sure. The whole thing's falling to pieces, but you're right—I'm sure that young woman needs it, poor thing.'

He crouched down and peered under the low-slung chassis, and Toni, who had bent down at the same moment to inspect the damage, suddenly found her head level with the doctor's, just as she had that afternoon, looking out from under the tractor. Once again his amazing gentian-blue eyes stared straight into hers, and she caught her breath, astonished by their violet depths and the intense gleam of warmth and tenderness that burned in them.

Footsteps approached from across the gravel, and before they could unlock their eyes, Dr Meredith appeared beside the van. They both stood up, and turned bland faces towards him. The older man flicked a penetrating glance at each of them, and they knew he had sensed the tension between them. What they didn't see was the look of compassion that he bestowed on them both.

'Can it be made good?' he asked Rupert, gesturing towards the van.

'Probably. The door wants fixing, but that's nothing. I think the steering's up the spout. It's something of a death-trap, but it's passed its MOT, apparently, and is taxed up to date. Most of all, Mrs White depends on it.'

'We'll contact Bob Wright at the garage tomorrow, get him to fix it.' Dr Meredith gave Toni and Rupert a ferocious look. 'Mrs White's little accident in the car park will be covered by our insurance, right?'

'Right,' agreed Rupert, grinning broadly.

Toni started to say something, then thought better of it. 'I'm so pleased that something can be done about the van,' she said quietly, giving both men a nice smile. 'Now I think I'd better be off. Grandfather will be wondering where I've got to and,' she gave Rupert a separate, cheeky smile, 'I'm under doctor's orders to start his treatment this evening.'

'Then off you go, my dear,' said Dr Meredith. 'And thanks for your help this evening. We couldn't have managed without you, could we, Rupert?'

Rupert shook his head and stepped forward to offer support as she leapt up into the driver's seat of the Land Rover. Toni almost, but didn't, shake off his helping hand.

'Thank you,' she said softly as she settled herself behind the wheel. Her eyes and his met briefly once again.

'Goodnight. Drive carefully,' said Rupert.

'OK, I will,' replied Toni, aware that something momentous had happened against the prosaic back-drop of the Health Centre car park.

Rupert and Dr Meredith watched her drive away into the dusky warmth of the May night. The sky was raspberry-red and ultramarine to the west, where the sun had set. They walked slowly side by side across the almost empty tarmac towards the Centre building. Both were silent, deep in thought.

As they reached the door, Rupert stood aside to let the older man pass through. They halted in the dim light of the entrance hall and surveyed each other.

Rupert gave a quirky, uncertain smile and shrugged. 'Well, Morris?' he asked, well aware that his companion had noted what had passed between him and Toni.

Dr Meredith said quietly, 'Antonia King is a lovely girl, but she's been bruised and battered by events in the last year. Even her close friends tread carefully where her emotions are concerned.'

'Are you warning me off?'

'Why, is there any reason to do so?' asked the other man blandly.

'You're very perceptive, Morris, I think you read the situation out there.' Rupert jerked his head towards the park. 'The thing is, I feel such a bloody fool. Here I am at thirty-eight falling for someone years younger—and not only in years, she's innocent and vulnerable.'

'Well, you know what they say about a late love, old chap. It tends to be the real thing and can be a painful business.' Morris turned and walked across the reception area. 'You know, Rupert, Toni may not be quite as innocent as you think, but she's certainly vulnerable. Go warily. I don't want to see either of you get hurt. I have an affection for you both. Your father was my best friend, and I adored Toni's grandmother, though she was ten years my senior.'

Rupert felt a great wave of compassion for the older man. 'Morris, I had no idea. You must still be grieving for her. She died only recently, I understand.'

'Yes,' said Dr Meredith bleakly. He squared his shoulders. 'Well, we can't stay here all night, better get home to supper.'

Toni drove home from the Centre in a curiously elated mood, thrilled that she had been useful in the surgery, knowing she had surmounted a personal hurdle by

overcoming the fears and self-deprecation of the past
months.

She hardly dared think of what had passed so silently
between her and Rupert Devenish. Even now, against
all the evidence to the contrary, she half wondered if
she had imagined the look in his eyes when they met
hers, a compound of compassion, understanding and
love, but not, she was convinced, romantic, sexual
love. He was a married man with a family, and
obviously content with his life—that had been the first
thing she had noticed about him, that and a kind of
transparent honesty and kindness.

No one with qualities like that would set out to
deceive. And if he had, surely she would not have felt
so instinctively safe with him. He would not have
inspired her with more confidence in a few hours than
her loving grandmother and friends had been able to
achieve in months.

It was quite clear that the extraordinary sensation
that had passed between them was rooted in a deeper,
more complex emotion than sexual attraction. Time
would determine what that was; for the moment she
was content to wallow in the first feelings of freedom
from fear, shame and outrage with which she had lived
for nearly a year.

She had Dr Rupert Devenish to thank for that, and
the calm strength that emanated from him, which he
seemed to have directed at her.

She felt great!

CHAPTER FOUR

TONI arrived back at Timbers still in an elated state, sufficiently buoyed up to deflect her grandfather's anger at the delay in giving him his treatment, and his supper.

'I'm sorry I'm late,' she said cheerfully. 'But there was an accident down at the Health Centre when I went to collect your medicine, and I got involved.'

'How did you get involved? Plenty of people there to look after patients, I'd have thought. That's what they're supposed to do, isn't it?'

'I am a nurse, Grandpa, and I just happened to be there at the time. You wouldn't want me not to do my duty, would you?'

She knew this would put him on the spot, since duty and honour were paramount virtues in his book.

He agreed in a grumbling fashion that she was right to put duty first, but remained irritable all the while she was treating his ulcerated leg.

'Why,' he complained, 'did Morris Meredith send that young whippersnapper to see me?'

'He's not so young' Toni explained. 'He must be in his late thirties at least. And he's an expert on tissue damage, and this new treatment may do the trick and heal your ulcer.'

'Not before time,' said the brigadier, still grumpy. He switched his interest suddenly, and asked, 'What sort of mess are you giving me for supper?'

'Shepherd's pie, followed by banana custard. Your favourites, Grandpa.' He had reverted in recent years to a schoolboy diet.

'Hmm. I don't know why Klemp and Mrs Klemp

have to have a day off.' He sounded vague and
genuinely puzzled.

'Because they have to have at least one day off a
week—you know that. And you're not in the Army
now, and Klemp isn't your batman any more, and Mrs
Klemp's a saint to look after us the way she does.'

She was never quite sure whether her grandfather
had forgotten that the war and his Army days were
over, or if he just used his occasional and apparent
confusion to get his own way.

'What's this chap's name?' the old man asked
suddenly.

'Which chap, Grandpa?'

'Doctor feller whom Morris sent.'

'Dr Rupert Devenish.'

Toni stood up, having secured the dressing in place
on the ulcerated leg. She was glad the light was dim
out of range of the table lamp, and that her grandfather's eyes were not as all-seeing as they used to be.
She felt the blood rushing to her cheeks as she spoke;
somehow, even saying the name Rupert Devenish
affected her, made her feel better. Better than she had
felt for a long time. Safe somehow, though she couldn't
explain why, even to herself.

With neat, precise movements she cleared away the
debris left over from cleaning and dressing the ulcer.
The high colour that only she was aware of faded from
her cheeks.

'Come on, Grandpa, let's have supper,' she said in
her usual calm manner.

She had a wonderful night's sleep, and woke feeling
light-hearted and happy. It was astonishing to think
that meeting one person, a stranger whom she might
never see again, could reverse the depression and guilt
of the last few months.

It had, though, just as her counsellor, Dr Ranji, had suggested that some such incident might.

'Suddenly,' she'd said, in her soft musical voice, 'you might wake up and find you've shed your guilt, your depression, associated with what happened. Such things are possible. Your sadness at your grand-mother's death might not go away for a long time, and is quite different. But that's natural, endurable, and will fade as time passes.'

Toni found herself walking over to the nursery after breakfast, eager to start work, eager to get on with what she felt in her bones was going to be a wonderful day.

There was dew on the grass and on the dark needles of the stately cupressus that lined the drive. The air smelt deliciously fresh after yesterday's storm. The early morning sun was shining, and warmed her bare brown legs and arms. She actually found herself skip-ping down the drive, and singing with the sheer joy of being alive. The awful burden that she had carried around with her for so long really had disappeared. She was free as air.

'And all thanks to you, Dr Rupert Devenish,' she said out loud, and experienced a small pang at the thought that she might not see him again. He's just passing through, Bridget had said. Oh, well, that was a pity, but nothing could spoil her present elation. Dr Devenish had been the catalyst that had freed her. It would have been nice to get to know him better, but he wasn't necessary to her future.

A future full of all the small pleasures that her own response to what had happened had denied her over the last few months.

She would become involved again with her old set around and about the village. Bridget and other friends, who had been patient and caring, would welcome her back into the fold. It would be difficult initially, but she would do it.

It was cool, almost too cool in the seed shed at this early hour. The phone rang as she went in. It would be the shop manager wanting supplies before they opened.

She lifted the receiver.

'Hello, Harry,' she sang out happily. 'How can I help you?'

'Well, you do sound happy, Miss King,' said a deep voice in her ear.

Toni was conscious of her heart thumping madly and her cheeks tingling. With difficulty she controlled the slight stutter that had plagued her since she was a child when she was frightened or caught unawares.

'I'm s-sorry,' she said primly. 'I thought it was the manager ringing from the shop.'

'It's Rupert Devenish,' said the voice, telling her what she already knew.

'Oh, Dr Devenish, how nice to hear from you!' She wondered if her voice gave her away, and if he'd noticed how pleased and surprised she was to hear from him, and if it mattered if he had.

'I'm sorry to bother you so early,' he said, 'but yesterday, seeing all those lovely plants that you grow in your hothouses, I wondered if you might suggest something suitable for someone who's in hospital. A nicely scented plant that will survive the high temperatures that hospital rooms have to maintain.'

'Well,' Toni just stopped herself from stuttering again, 'there are many to choose from in the shop. They'll advise you.'

As soon as she said it she realised that it was not what she wanted to say. She was deliberately preventing him from coming to the nursery, perhaps preventing herself from seeing him for the last time. What on earth had made her do such a thing?

'Ah,' he said softly, 'I should go to the shop and look for something there?' There was a question and a hint of surprise in his voice.

'Y-yes—well, no not really. What I mean is, you don't have to. I can help you choose a plant here, at the nursery. I do sell things direct.'

'That's what I thought,' said Dr Devenish. He was now firm, decisive. 'May I call in later and have the benefit of your advice?'

'Of course, any time,' Toni said softly, breathlessly.

She replaced the receiver and did a little dance on the dirt floor of the seed-room. She had been happy enough when she came to work, but for some reason, which she didn't care to examine, Dr Devenish's phone call had further exhilarated her. She was on top of the world. She would be seeing him again.

Bridget phoned later.

'We've had an impromptu staff meeting,' she said in her bubbly sort of voice. 'And guess what? Our gorgeous Dr Devenish is going to stay put for a while. He's going to continue to work here as well as do his lecture stuff in London. Dr Meredith's over the moon about it, he's not been too well lately and I think he's glad to have someone so experienced to share the load with.'

Toni, who was pricking out tiny seedlings, and had hurried to the phone with a tray of minuscule plantlets in her hand, disguised the wave of pleasure that the news gave her by saying rather briskly, 'Good, I'm pleased for you.' She added, 'Look, Bridget, I'm very busy at the moment, I'll ring you back.'

'Don't do that, come to the tennis club tonight. Terry and I are going to be there, and some of the old gang. They'd love to see you.'

'Well, I'm not sure.'

A couple of days ago, before meeting Rupert

Devenish, she would have flatly refused. She hadn't socialised for nearly a year. Even Granny hadn't been able to persuade her to go out and about. Now things were different. Last night she had found the courage to put on a dress to go to the Health Centre, and not jeans or culottes as had become the norm when she left home ground. A small thing, but a giant step forward for her. She had half expected Bridget to comment on the fact, but she hadn't. Perhaps it was only of significance to herself.

'Oh, go on, be a devil!' Bridget was pleading in a soft voice. 'Your grandmother would have wanted you to give it a try—you know that. And you're a great player, Toni, you should start again. After all, you've got to begin some time, and the divine Devenish might be there, signing up for membership, now he's going to be a resident in Peckhurst. According to dear old Doc Meredith, he's at least county class.'

Toni knew that this last piece of information, on top of her new-found reassurance, was the deciding factor.

'Yes, you're right—I must start getting back into circulation soon. OK, I'll be there. What time?'

'Oh, that's great. I thought I might persuade you— you were wearing that smashing yellow dress for the first time in ages, last evening. I hoped it might mean you're on the mend. I'm so glad, Toni. As to time, about eight. We're sorting out eliminating matches for the end-of-season tournament.'

'Right—see you.' Toni hesitated slightly, then added, 'I'm glad you noticed—about the dress.'

Bridget laughed. 'Couldn't miss it, and I am by way of being your best friend. It was quite a breakthrough, wasn't it?'

She rang off.

Tony went back to work, lifting, with delicate precision, the tiny two-leaved seedlings from the tray of hundreds. She set their hair-like threads of roots into pots of specially prepared culture soil. Within days they would shoot up and produce further leaves, strengthen their root systems, and become recognisable species. Nurtured carefully, they would continue to flourish until they were an inch or two taller, and ready to be potted on yet again.

'A long and loving process,' she could hear Granny saying. 'But so worthwhile, helping germinating seeds to life.' This rather whimsical sort of comment would usually be followed by a very practical remark about manure and soil analysis and suchlike. And this was often the signal for Mrs King, elegant in corduroy breeches, to hop on the tractor and spend an hour or so hauling sacks of fertiliser, or something equally heavy, over the Rise.

Grandmother had been a mixture of the practical and the poet, thought Toni, smiling at the thought. She willed herself to concentrate on the fiddly job of transplanting the seedlings, and ignore the thrill of pleasure that the news of Rupert's intention to stay in Peckhurst produced.

Ever since last night when she had driven away from the surgery, leaving him and Dr Meredith standing in the car park, he seemed to have taken up residence in her mind. Then she had thought she might not see him again, and had not been particularly bothered about the possibility. But somewhere between their initial meeting and his phone call this morning, a desire to know him better, to build on their brief acquaintanceship, had begun to form.

It wasn't on the basis of man-met-woman, more a person-to-person relationship she hoped to achieve. She smiled inwardly at these rather grand thoughts, but knew what she meant and hoped that such a friendship might come about.

The phone rang stridently, cutting through her thoughts, making her jump. Simultaneously a car swished across the gravel and halted outside the seed-room. She knew at once that the visitor was Rupert Devenish, even though the car, which was partly visible through the open door, was not the one he had driven yesterday.

She picked up the phone, and, before she could speak, an agitated voice at the other end, said, 'Come quickly—there's been an accident on the Rise.'

The phone went dead before she could ask for any details.

Rupert was easing himself out of the dark blue Rover saloon, as Toni erupted through the doorway.

'Can you take me over the Rise?' she asked. 'There's been an accident.'

'Of course.' He moved back into the car and leaned over to open the passenger door. 'What's happened?'

'I don't know—the young chap who phoned rang off before I could ask. He sounded pretty scared, but it might not be too serious. You know how a little blood goes a long way.'

'Yes indeed.' Rupert smiled sideways at her as they took the dirt and grass track up the hill between the plantation of Christmas trees. 'You obviously look after the first-aid side of things here.'

'Yes, since my grandmother died. I used to help her, of course, when I started working full time in the nursery. She was a qualified first-aider with the St John's Ambulance.'

Now, thought Rupert, might be the occasion to ask in a casual fashion what had made her leave hospital, get her to tell him her version of events—except, he realised as they topped the Rise, there wasn't time.

About halfway down the slope leading to the garden shop and extensive greenhouses, a tractor was lying on its side. Beside it stood a young man who started to wave madly at them as soon as they appeared. From the direction of the shop, several people were running up the hill.

They went down the hill very fast, but, even in the few moments that it took them to cover the route to the overturned tractor, Toni sensed the strength with which the doctor controlled the car. He didn't waste a minute, and yet she felt safe in the speeding vehicle. As they neared the accident spot, he slewed carefully off the track, halting parallel with the stranded machine.

He lifted his medical case from the rear seat and was out of the car while she was still opening the passenger door.

He hardly paused as he said something to the young man, whom Toni recognised as Steve Morgan. Toni heard him say 'Ambulance,' and saw Steve pressing the buttons on the mobile phone.

She joined the doctor round the far side of the tractor. Half in and half out of the plastic cabin lay an older man with grey hair, whom she recognised at once.

'It's Jack Deal,' she said. 'Is he. . .?'

Dr Devenish was crouching down beside the man. He was feeling for a pulse in the man's temple, the easiest part to reach, as one arm lay at a grotesque angle, trapped beneath a huge wheel, and the other was concealed beneath his body. Blood was oozing from a superficial cut on his head.

'Faint, thready, but there's something. Open my bag, please, and fish out my stethoscope.' With controlled but slightly trembling fingers Toni handed him the instrument. 'Thanks.'

'What else do you want me to do?'

'Ask the young man with the phone to contact the fire brigade. We're going to need lifting gear for this.' He nodded at the huge iron framework of the tractor.

Toni relayed the message about the fire engine to Steve Morgan.

Harry Yates, the manager, who had just arrived puffing, with others from the shop, said breathlessly, 'We can lift it, we've got some gear.'

'No!' said Dr Devenish sharply. 'Don't touch anything, you may do more harm than good.' He softened his words and manner by flashing Harry a brief smile. 'You can send someone for blankets, anything to keep this chap warm.'

'Right.' Harry said something to two men standing by, and they hurried off down the hill.

Wendy Shaw, the senior shop assistant, arrived on the scene.

'Anything I can do?' she asked Toni.

'I don't know, Dr Devenish is assessing the situation. Just stay put for a bit.'

'OK.'

Toni, still crouching next to the doctor, waited for him to give her further instructions. He finished moving his stethoscope about over Jack Deal's chest, and lifted each eyelid to examine the pupils for levels of unconsciousness.

'I'm worried about his back,' he said softly. 'I'm going to have a feel around, to see if there are any internal injuries. While I'm doing that, you have a look at his legs, see if they're badly damaged or might be released. Then draw up a two-mil ampoule of Pethilorfan, which you'll find in the top right-hand compartment of my case, together with syringes.'

Toni crawled across to the cabin of the tractor. The hugely thick wheels had prevented it from touching the ground by a few inches. The door had evidently burst open as his body fell from the driver's seat, but had half closed again as the machine toppled over. She could just about squeeze through enough to examine his legs. One was at a peculiar angle, the other was just bent, the knee against the door as if propping it open.

She crawled back to the doctor's side. He was looking grim.

'Internal bleeding—I'm sure of it,' he mouthed at her, obviously not wanting the watchers to hear. 'What about his legs?'

'Both fractured, I think, one a femur, judging by the angle of the limb, the other a tib and fib, no skin broken to speak of but swelling and bruising over the shin.'

Toni drew up the ampoule of Pethilorfan as she spoke, and showed him the small vial and the syringe so that he could check contents and quantity.

He nodded and took the syringe from her, but kept the cover on the needle.

'I'll give it as soon as he starts regaining consciousness,' he said, and gave her a smile. 'Let's hope the ambulance people get here soon. This poor chap's going to need high-powered care, I'm afraid.'

As he finished speaking a siren sounded coming from the top of the Rise, and an ambulance appeared and drove steadily down the slope towards them. Within minutes a fire engine, klaxons wailing, climbed up the hill from the direction of the shop.

'Thank God!' breathed Dr Devenish, smiling again at Toni. 'The cavalry have arrived. Now we're in business!'

A casualty officer had come out with the ambulance crew. This apparently was the drill at the local hospital when a victim was trapped beneath a vehicle and might need prolonged attention before being released.

He had a conversation with Rupert, and together they re-examined poor Jack Deal, who was just showing signs of coming round. The casualty officer agreed that a shot of painkiller, in this case the Pethilorfan already drawn up, would be advisable. Once it was given, Rupert withdrew.

Toni had already handed over to the ambulance crew and was standing talking to Harry Yates and Wendy Shaw.

'Just enter it in the accident book,' she told Harry, 'in the usual way. But make a note that Dr Devenish and I arrived on the scene first. Leave a space for us to enter any information about Jack's condition. I'll sort it out with the doctor. Note that the ambulance and fire brigade were called, and get the approximate time from Steve Morgan, and also get a statement from him as to what happened. I'll come over later and go through it with you.'

She gave the usually very self-sufficient manager a reassuring smile, sensing that this accident was rather out of the usual run-of-the-mill occasions.

'Shall I organise teas or something?' asked Wendy. 'It looks as if this lot will be here for some time.'

'Good idea, and make sure Steve has something. He's had a hell of a shock and needs a stimulant like a hot, sweet drink.'

'OK, will do,' said Wendy, and made for the shop at the bottom of the hill.

Rupert touched Toni's arm. 'I've got to go,' he said. 'I'm way behind on my visits, and I'm afraid the plant will have to wait. But I can run you back to the nursery.'

Much as she wanted to go with him, Toni refused. For the first time since her grandmother's death she realised that someone had to take her place in the running of King's Seeds, and that she was the obvious candidate. Even Harry Yates had welcomed her advice and support, and Wendy had deferred to her in the matter of instructions about serving refreshments to the rescue people. A small thing, but somehow important.

'No, thanks,' she said, refusing not only the politely worded offer but the invitation apparent in his intensely blue eyes. 'I've got to stay around here. But I would be grateful for an opportunity to talk some time. Harry Yates needs our statement about the accident for his records.'

'Of course.' He eased her away from the crowd. 'Are you sure you're all right?' He squeezed her arm gently. 'It must have been a nasty shock for you—not just an accident, they're always distressing, but knowing the people involved, and of course being more or less their employer.'

Rather surprised at her own reaction, Toni said firmly, 'I'm fine, but I can't thank you enough for your help. It would have been much more difficult without you.'

'Glad to have been of service,' he replied, in a light, almost teasing voice. 'I'll give you a ring, if I may, about the statement and so on.'

'Thanks.' If only he knew, she thought, how much more help he had given, other than providing professional expertise at the accident. Unknowingly, he had made her into a new and responsible woman.

She watched him drive down the wide track and disappear round the conglomeration of buildings that formed the shop complex.

Rupert, giving what attention he was forced to to the rough track, watched her, as he had the day before, in his mirror. There she stood, a silver-blonde beauty, looking young, vulnerable, and, from his point of view, utterly desirable. Of course, he now possessed information about her to which he had not been privy the previous day. But what he had heard from Morris Meredith had only made him more determined to befriend and, in time, enter into a closer, more romantic association with Antonia King. But he knew she would need time. Time to come to terms with her new-found confidence, and, even more so, time to consider a close relationship with any man.

Well, he decided, he could be both patient and determined.

CHAPTER FIVE

TONI was frantically busy for the rest of the day, organising shop and nursery matters to continue with as little interruption as possible, in spite of the accident.

She went personally to tell Jack Deal's wife what had happened, then took her to the hospital. Fortunately she was able to contact the Deals' daughter and leave Mrs Deal in her care when she herself returned to the shop.

There were various officials to be dealt with, including a safety-at-work officer; and support to be given to young Steve Morgan when he gave his version of the accident and the events leading up to it. From what Steve said, and from what Dr Devenish and the casualty officer had discovered on examination, it seemed likely that Jack had suffered a heart attack. Both the medical men would be asked to give statements to confirm what might have been the cause of the accident.

It was late afternoon before Toni was able to leave the shop, return to the manor house and break the news of the accident to her grandfather. She would rather have kept it from him altogether, but knew that inevitably he would hear rumours, which would be more worrying than hearing the truth from her.

She told him what had happened over a cup of tea served on the veranda on the south side of the house. He looked less frail today, Toni thought, which meant he would be better able to tolerate the news, but was more likely to be explosive about it.

He was. 'What?' he shouted in his parade-ground

voice, extraordinarily strong considering his years. 'An accident, and someone's been badly hurt? How did it happen? The driver must have been bloody careless! Where did it happen, and who was the driver?'

'The driver was Jack Deal, and you know how careful he is. The doctors think he may have had a heart attack and lost control as he turned on the Rise.'

'Jack Deal—poor feller.' The brigadier's temper subsided as quickly as it had arisen. 'Well, he's sensible enough. Been with us—what, twenty years or so?'

'Yes.'

'What about Mrs Deal, does she know what's happened?'

'I went to see her and took her to the hospital. Her daughter's with her now. I couldn't stay any longer, there was such a lot to do back here, all sorts of officials to see, and I had to notify the insurance people, as well as reassure the staff. Everyone was rather shaken by what had happened.'

'And what was your uncle Jeremy doing while all this was happening?' The brigadier's voice was icy with contempt as he questioned her about his eldest son. There was certainly no love lost between them, and never had been, and though Toni had little respect for her uncle she felt rather sorry for him at times. Her grandfather could be scathing and quite unforgiving.

'He's away for a couple of days. Don't you remember, Grandpa, he had to go up to town to discuss a large shipment of seeds with a Japanese firm.'

'Hmph, more likely womanising,' growled the brigadier in his old-fashioned way. 'You going to get in touch with him? After all, he is supposed to be the managing director of King's Seeds.'

'He's due back tomorrow; there's no point in trying to get hold of him now.'

'Well, I think you should. He ought to be told.'

'No, Grandpa,' Toni surprised herself by her own

firmness. 'It's pointless, there's nothing he can do.' In fact, she thought privately, he would do more harm than good, blustering about and blaming everyone for what had happened. Before the old gentleman could protest further, she added, 'I'm going to phone the hospital now, see if there's any more news about Jack. You stay here for a while, then we'll have a stroll round the garden before I see to the dressing on your leg.'

Her grandfather opened his mouth to say something in his usual dictatorial manner, but the expression on her face, and the determined set of her lips, stopped him. Instead, he watched her disappear through the french doors leading from the veranda into the small sitting-room, and guessed she was phoning the hospital from there.

Jack Deal was still in the intensive care unit. He was being monitored and everything that could be done to make him comfortable was being done, the unit sister assured her.

To Toni's enquiry about Mrs Deal, she was told that yes, Mrs Deal and her daughter were still there, but no, it would be better if Miss King didn't visit again at present.

Toni went back to her grandfather and relayed the news to him.

'Funny goings-on,' he said fiercely to conceal his concern. 'Didn't they say if they'd fixed his legs or anything?'

'No, I expect they've immobilised them, but the most important thing at the moment is to stabilise his heart and try to stop the internal bleeding. Keep his blood and plasma levels up and give him painkillers. It's routine, Grandpa, I know, first things first—I've worked on ICU.'

She helped the old man up from his chair and handed him his stick. He straightened himself up in a dignified manner, almost to his full six feet, and gave her an affectionate smile.

'Toni,' he said, taking her arm as they descended the steps to the rose garden, 'you're a rather splendid young woman, nearly worthy of your granny, and like her in looks. You'll do, my gal, you'll do.'

The compliment from her grandfather, who at best she loved with filial duty rather than true affection, overwhelmed her. She couldn't think of anything to say in response, and consequently babbled away about the roses being at their midsummer best, until they finished their walk.

It was a little after eight o'clock when she arrived at the tennis club, having done battle with herself about whether to go or not in the circumstances. But it was ridiculous to stay mooning around at home. She had to break the social ice some time, and there was nothing more she could do at present to help the Deals.

Bridget, with her husband Terry, was sitting on the terrace overlooking the courts.

'Over here,' she called to Toni.

Toni threaded her way between the chairs and tables, and was surprised to be greeted warmly by several people, who were obviously pleased to see her. It looked as if her first foray into society after her self-imposed exile would not be as frightening as she had anticipated. After all, only a few close friends knew what had actually happened in London; everyone else assumed that she had been ill, and now remained at Timbers to look after her grandfather following her grandmother's recent death.

There were several other people at the table— Kieron Duffry, a local architect, whom she had known quite well in the past, and Jill and Tom Langston who owned Bookworms, a paperback and secondhand bookshop in the town. At the next table, Melanie Bean—String Bean, she had been called as a girl, on account of her tall, willowy frame—was in close conversation with Dr Pat MacNiece, junior partner in the Health Centre practice.

Toni had known them both for years. They had all been at convent school together. Melanie was now a tall, sophisticated brunette beauty who sometimes graced the society pages of *Horse and Hound* or *Country Life*.

For a moment, Toni's confidence faltered. She had always admired Melanie's elegance and poise, and by comparison felt short, dumpy and colourless. Her newly found assurance had hardly prepared her for such a meeting. She almost turned tail and ran, but the greeting she received from both her old school friends restored her equilibrium. They were obviously pleased to see her. She'd forgotten that beneath the smooth exterior Melanie was a thoroughly nice person.

She took herself in hand, determined to enjoy her first real outing.

Of Dr Rupert Devenish there was no sign, and, though Toni realised that it was an outside chance that he would be there, she experienced a small pang of disappointment at his absence.

Everyone seemed pleased to see her. It was surprising how quickly she found herself talking to them, one after another, having prepared herself to find it difficult to make casual conversation.

Of course, the accident at the nursery helped—they had all heard about it and wanted details from someone who was there at the time. But their curiosity was friendly rather than morbid, since Jack Deal was known to most of them and they were concerned for his welfare.

'What'll you drink?' asked Terry Banks soon after Toni had sat down. 'We're all having spritzers, very mild alcohol-wise at this time of the evening, but we'll go on to fruit juice or mineral water later as most of us are driving.'

'Lovely! I'll have a spritzer too.'

Kieron Duffry was very attentive.

'Nice to have you back,' he said. 'What about you and I having a go at the mixed doubles first round? We used to be quite good together, remember?'

Toni recalled that they had played together some years before. He had been rather a spotty, pallid youth then, a year or two her senior. Now he looked handsome and confident, with his thick fair hair brushed neatly back from a broad forehead, and his bronzed face and arms looking strong and muscular. He had done quite well professionally too, she'd heard, his firm winning a competition for the design of a hospital complex up north. It might be fun getting to know him all over again.

'Well, that might be possible,' she replied cautiously, not quite sure where she stood in the tennis club hierarchy after her absence. 'As I remember, you had a particularly good backhand.'

'And you a magnificent serve and volley.'

'Great, all we need is to improve our forehand and service returns and we're in with a chance, then.'

They smiled at each other, completely in accord.

'You betcha,' said Kieron in a joking fashion, and leaned over to punch Toni's arm lightly in a friendly gesture, just as Dr Meredith and Rupert Devenish appeared on the terrace.

'There,' murmured Bridget, 'I said he might come.'

'So you did,' agreed Toni, suppressing the wave of excitement that threatened to overwhelm her and make her blush. She was glad she had put on the navy blue cotton dress with the scooped-out neckline and big splashy poppy pattern. The dark material enhanced her silver-blondeness and golden tan, and the brilliant flowers matched her carefree mood. She forgot that only minutes before she had compared herself to Melanie and found herself wanting.

The two doctors joined their group, pulling over chairs from an adjacent table. Somebody fetched them drinks, and Dr Meredith introduced his colleague to Kieron and one or two others who hadn't so far met him.

After a few polite preliminaries with those to whom he had just been introduced, Rupert shuffled his chair along until he was next to Toni. Kieron, on her other side, frowned as if he resented Rupert's nearness.

'Dr Devenish. . .' he began.

'Rupert, please.'

Kieron gave him a tight smile. 'Rupert, Toni and I,' he put an arm round Toni's shoulder, 'are old friends. We used to partner each other in the junior championships, and we're going to have a go at club level this year.' It was quite clear to an astonished Toni that he was staking a claim. He gave her a beaming smile. 'And whack them hollow, darling, aren't we?'

Toni felt trapped. She wished he would remove his hand from her shoulder. It was burning through the thin cotton of her dress. It was the first close contact with a man that she'd had since. . .

I can do without this, she thought, and tried to control her breathing, which was becoming fast and shallow. It seemed natural that she should look with pleading eyes at Rupert, knowing, though she didn't know how, that he would understand what was happening to her.

He leaned forward and stared straight into Kieron's brown eyes.

'Well, we'll have to see about that.' He paused, and transferred his gaze to Toni. 'Antonia,' his use of her full name surprised her, and even Kieron looked momentarily startled, 'I was rather under the impression that you and I were in partnership.' He looked at her with a bland expression in his deep blue eyes, daring her to call his bluff.

Kieron dropped his arm from Toni's shoulder. 'You didn't say anything about this,' he said angrily, glaring at her. 'Anyway, you've got to be a member to compete.' This last was said triumphantly to Rupert.

'Ah, yes—well, Dr Meredith has signed me in as an honorary member pro tem, as I'm staying in the district, with full membership in three months' time. Apparently this allows me to compete in this year's championships.'

Kieron turned an angry face to Toni. 'You might have told me!' he said, and, pushing back his chair noisily, left the table.

Toni felt awful. True, she had wanted Rupert to do something to make Kieron stop fondling her, but she hadn't wanted to hurt him.

'Kieron!' she called to his retreating back, but he ignored her and left the terrace.

The flow of conversation went on around her and Rupert continued talking as if nothing had happened. Nobody seemed to have noticed Kieron's sudden departure, or at least the reason for it.

Dr Meredith was speaking. 'Rupert will be a great asset,' he said. 'He's played at county level in the past in singles and mixed doubles—isn't that so, Rupert?'

'For my sins, yes, Morris, but I'm rather out of practice this season, especially for singles,' said Rupert. 'I might have a go at the doubles, with the right partner.'

Bridget said quickly, 'Toni used to be a splendid doubles player. Perhaps you ought to give it a try together.' She produced an innocent smile aimed at both of them.

'Well, I'm game, if Antonia is,' said Rupert, again using her full name deliberately, almost challenging her to take him up on it. He looked her straight in the eye. 'In fact, we were just talking about the possibility, weren't we?'

Somehow she managed a natural smile.

'Yes, I prefer doubles to singles. Like Dr Devenish, I'm rather out of practice, and might do better with a partner.'

'Great,' said Terry Banks, scribbling on his note-pad. 'Let's make that a definite yes for the first round.' He turned to Melanie Bean, and quite innocently, unaware of the little drama that had just taken place at their table, suggested, 'And what about you, Mel, getting together with Kieron? You're both good play-ers, and if I put you two in one half of the draw, and Toni and Rupert in the other, we should be in for a good final.'

He beamed at everyone, and Melanie blushed. Toni, slowly recovering her calm, noted this with interest. Could it be possible that the gorgeous Melanie fancied Kieron? It certainly looked that way. Perhaps, thought Toni, despising herself for the thought, I'm not a complete washout. I can still provide a bit of competition.

She was conscious of Rupert sitting close beside her.

'Are you game,' he asked, his gentian-blue eyes twinkling, 'for a game? I'd be honoureed if you'd partner me, new member that I am.' He managed to project an image of a humble beginner, which made her laugh. 'That's better,' he said, 'but will you partner me, Antonia?'

'Why not?' She had to say something more, and added softly, 'Thank you for coming to the rescue. I— I'll explain some time.'

'No need,' he said. 'I understand.' His blue, so very blue eyes, bored into hers, and she knew he did understand, though how she wasn't sure.

The evening continued on its predictable course,

with a lot of laughing and teasing as draws for places in the first round of the matches were planned out. From time to time other members joined them, and gradually, towards eleven o'clock, people started to drift away home.

Toni, bemused and happy and at last at peace with herself, even allowing for the minor upset of Kieron's precipitate departure, decided that she must leave.

'I must go,' she said to Rupert, who had remained by her side for the entire evening. 'Grandpa likes me to say goodnight to him, and I'm not usually so late.'

'No, I don't suppose you are, as you don't often go out, do you?' Rupert put out a tentative hand and touched hers as it lay on the table.

Toni took a few deep breaths. She didn't feel threatened by his hand on hers. She smiled at him uncertainly, and shook her head.

'No,' she whispered, 'I don't.'

'But you'll start coming regularly for practice, won't you?'

She nodded. 'Yes.'

'Good. See you tomorrow about seven.'

'Yes.'

'By the way,' Rupert added, 'I've given my statement to the powers that be about the accident. Poor Mr Deal—I rang the hospital this evening just before Morris and I left the surgery to enquire about his progress. You'd phoned shortly before, I believe, and nothing's changed much, though they're going to put him into limited traction tonight, to improve the fracture condition of his legs. And they think they've controlled the internal bleed, so things look more hopeful.' He gave her a strange look, as if he were uncertain of himself, which didn't match his usual confident state. 'I should have told you sooner, but you seemed happy, I didn't want to spoil it with talking shop.'

'Oh, I'm so glad there's an improvement. Thank you for telling me. It doesn't matter that you waited till now.' She felt herself blushing again, and stammering, 'In—in f-fact, it was k-kind of you.'

'Not at all,' he said, sounding rather formal and pushing back his chair to stand up beside her as she prepared to leave. He looked deep into her eyes, and it was as if they were alone despite the babble of conversation which was going on around them. 'Whatever I can do, now or at any time, Antonia, you have only to ask.'

'Yes, I know,' she heard herself reply, and knew it was true. Rupert Devenish was her friend and comforter, her rock. She had the overwhelming sense of being cherished, cared for. She never had to feel alone or at risk ever again.

She drove home in much the same state of euphoria as on the previous evening, her thoughts almost entirely concentrated on Rupert Devenish. She sat for a few minutes in the Land Rover when she drew up in front of the manor house, mulling over the day, and particularly the evening.

It was sad, she reflected, that it had taken two accidents to bring about the minor miracle of her recovery from shock and fear. Then she recapitulated and admitted that, though these traumatic incidents had speeded matters up, it was her meeting with Rupert Devenish that had started the ball rolling towards her recovery.

He was, as she had privately admitted before, the lynchpin of her return to normality, and every encounter with him since that initial meeting had further cemented the fact. He seemed to have second sight where she and her difficulties were concerned. He was capable of picking up her reactions to a situation with surprising speed and accuracy. Like tonight, when she had nearly panicked because Kieron had kept his hand on her arm too long, too suggestively. Rupert had quickly and positively dealt with that event, concerned only to relieve her of her anxiety.

His reading of her reaction to Kieron's possessive action was quite extraordinary. Was it because he was a good and concerned doctor, had that given him a greater insight into her state of mind? Probably she would never know, just as she might never know any more about his personal or home life. He seemed to be a very free agent, able to opt, as far as she knew from what Bridget had told her, at short notice, to stay in Peckhurst and commute to town when necessary. He must have a docile, undemanding wife, or a very independent one.

The idea of Dr Devenish either in the bosom of his family, or ready to separate himself from it at a moment's notice, was thought-provoking. Thoughts that kept her from sleep until the small hours.

They were puzzling, tantalising. Why, she wondered, was a man who seemed so good and reliable prepared to spend time away from his family? Why had he joined the tennis club and offered to partner her for the championships? How was it he was able to convince her that his friendship was an important factor in her complete recovery, and all without specific words on the subject?

There was, she decided, only one person apart from Rupert Devenish himself who might come up with some of the answers: Dr Meredith—Uncle Morris, as she had called him when she was a child. He must know something about this enigmatic man whom he had engaged to assist him in the practice. According to Bridget he had known Rupert's father—a slender thread, perhaps, but it could mean that he might be able and willing to provide her with information about the son of his old friend.

Of course, if Granny were alive, she could have persuaded Dr Meredith to tell her anything, as long as it didn't interfere with doctor-patient confidentiality.

On the verge of sleep at last, confident that she could learn something more about Rupert Devenish, Toni pondered on the relationship that had flourished between Dr Meredith and her grandmother. It had been close and special, she knew, in spite of the difference in their ages, and that, as some would consider, the wrong way round. But as far as Toni knew, Granny had remained a devoted wife to Grandpa till the end.

Her heavy eyelids closed at last on the traumatic and emotional day as she thought of her grandparents and Dr Meredith. The three of them had remained friends, and the doctor was even now her grandfather's closest friend and companion. Of course, they were of a generation that believed in the marriage vows, and 'till death us do part' meant precisely that.

Blurrily, through remnants of consciousness, she wondered what she would do if. . .

The thought died as she at last fell into a deep, profound sleep.

CHAPTER SIX

THE following day passed in a blur of hyperactivity.

News from the hospital about Jack Deal was good. He had stabilised overnight, and had stopped bleeding internally. He was still on a glucose and saline drip, but he was not now requiring IV blood. The ICU sister was willing for Toni to visit later in the day.

Uncle Jeremy came home late morning. As Toni had feared, he simply blustered about and blamed everyone from Harry Yates to herself for the accident.

The brigadier heard that he was back and sent Klemp to fetch him up to the manor house. He was rather subdued when he returned to his office behind the shop complex, passing on a message to Toni that her grandfather was waiting to have his ulcer attended to.

Toni went up to Timbers immediately. She removed the previous night's dressing, ignoring the old man's grumbles.

'Well, that's greatly improved!' she exclaimed, examining the wound, which for the first time in weeks loked clean and showed signs of granulating. 'It's just as Dr Devenish predicted,' she said. 'He thought it would be healing by today. He certainly knows his job. Now, Grandpa, I'm going to put on a new dressing, but unless you have any pain or discomfort it will be able to remain in situ for at least three days.'

'Hmmph, another of these modern miracle cures, I suppose,' muttered the brigadier grumpily. 'And saves a lot of time. Labour-saving, I dare say they call it. You won't have to come near me at all now if you don't want to.' He scowled at Toni as she bent over

65

his leg, douching it clean with the special lotion that the doctor had prescribed.

She didn't answer at once. Her new-found confidence in herself was extending, to her surprise, to her elderly relative. His comment yesterday evening about her likeness to her grandmother had been very revealing.

He had admired, virtually worshipped his wife, who had been one of the few people in his long life able to stand up to him, and even influence him. Toni could see that, old and frail as he now was, he really needed someone as strong as Granny had been to guide him through each day. Behaving as a fierce, irascible old tyrant was simply a façade behind which he hid. Now that she'd got his measure she would be able to form some sort of relationship with him without giving in to him all the time.

Perhaps in the process she could also assume a stronger role in the running of King's Seeds. She had a right as a family director to voice her opinions. After yesterday, when as the only King present she had exercised her authority, she felt able to do more than this. She knew she had handled matters far better than her uncle would have done. He would have made a complete hash of things, riding thoughtlessly over the feelings of the staff, and possibly even Mrs Deal. He simply wasn't any good at handling people. The money side of the business was all that he understood. Granny had always looked after the staff.

'We look after the people who work for us,' she had told Toni, 'because they're our friends as well as our employees, and they look after our customers. Like life in general, it's all a question of give and take. We all need each other.'

Toni finished securing the new dressing in place and smiled at her grandfather.

'Grandpa, we're going to spend plenty of time

together. Klemp can bring you down to the hothouses sometimes, and you and I can chat as I'm working. I should like that,' she added cunningly. 'It would be like working with Granny again.' She rushed on before he could interrupt and she lost her nerve, 'And what about doing an occasional inspection of the shop and packing sheds—a sort of parade? I'm sure the staff would appreciate you taking an interest in them. They do miss Granny.'

A range of expressions passed over the brigadier's face, leaving him looking drawn and pale. Toni wondered if she had gone too far. It was years since he had taken any active part in the firm, except for putting in an appearance at the staff Christmas party. Maybe her suggestion wasn't such a good one after all.

She put out a small tentative brown hand to touch him, and he grasped it in between his bony, veined, parchment-skinned fingers.

'A small hand, and a big heart, just like your granny's.' He managed a smile. 'Are you going to hustle me along like your late grandmama?'

'Of course—what else, Grandpa? I'm sure she's relying on me to do just that.' Toni stared at him defiantly, challenging him to force her to back off.

There were a few moments of almost unbearable silence before her grandfather spoke again.

'You're a worthy successor, my dear,' he said at last. 'In name and style.' To her astonishment, he bent forward and kissed her cheek. 'Good luck, Antonia, God bless you.'

Antonia. Granny was the only person who ever called her that. Granny, and, last night, Rupert Devenish. And now, quite suddenly, Grandpa was using her full female baptismal name. His late wife's second name, the wife after whom the young Antonia had been christened. Was this yet another watershed

in her life, another breakthrough arising since the
arrival of the charismatic doctor on the scene?

Toni sandwiched in a visit to the hospital between
organising a special display of flowers for the South-
down Show, the yearly agricultural and horticultural
show, an important three-day event in the local calen-
dar, and talking to reporters from the two local weekly
papers about the accident.

It was late afternoon before she got back to the
relative calm of the hothouses. The brilliance of the
morning, which had still worn a fresh-washed look
from the thunderstorm two days earlier, had passed,
and the sky was now a mass of yellow-grey clouds.
Thunder, like a muted drumroll, growled around the
horizon, following the contours of the rounded hills of
Sussex.

Letting herself into the seed house where the giant
fan performed its leisurely revolutions, Toni was struck
by the similarity to the afternoon of the storm on her
first meeting with Rupert Devenish. Now, as then,
there was a humid, heavy expectancy hanging over
everything. Then it had seemed all doom and gloom,
made worse by the atmospheric pressure, whereas
today, in spite of poor Jack and the accident, life had
a lift to it. Tonight she would be seeing Rupert, and
not in a professional context; tonight, even though she
was out of practice, she would play tennis with all the
panache she could muster.

She was re-potting some plants ready to be delivered
to the shop the following day when it suddenly came
to her that she hadn't a clue as to what she was going
to wear for her first practice match tonight. Was any
of her tennis gear fit to appear in? She hadn't had
dresses or shorts and shirts out to check this season.
They'd be clean, but would they need ironing and

freshening up, and if they did would she have time to do them before seven?

Of course, Mrs Klemp would see to them for her. She would be delighted that she was going to start playing again. Toni phoned the house kitchen.

'I don't like to ask you,' she apologised to the housekeeper. 'You've got enough to do, but would you be a dear and check out my tennis stuff and give anything that needs it a press? I'd be awfully grateful.'

'My dear Toni, you know I'm only too pleased to do something for you for a change. It's other people in this house who expect to be waited on hand and foot that I object to.'

Mrs Klemp disapproved of Uncle Jeremy and his wife Constance, who lived in a wing of the manor house. They entertained a lot, and most of their guests failed to reach the high standards that she set. She didn't try to disguise the fact. 'It's a cross I have to bear,' she would sometimes say. And as Granny King used to say, she bore it stoically, if not quietly.

Toni smiled to herself as she put down the phone and returned to her work. Mrs Klemp and her grandmother had been great friends.

It was nearly seven before Toni left home. It was just as well that she had asked for help, as she had been late leaving the nursery attending to all sorts of irritating jobs that couldn't be left till the following day. Normally she didn't mind how late she worked; work had become a solace and a solution to her self-imposed loneliness.

Now all that was suddenly changed. She was looking forward to the evening immensely. Last night had proved to her that she still had the friendship of her old circle at the club, and there was the pleasure in store of getting to know new members, and—she tried

in vain to squash the thought—one new member in
particular.

In spite of the heat, and the lowering clouds threatening rain, she looked and felt cool in her pristine
white shorts and plain cotton shirt. She had put on the
merest touch of make-up, a whisper of blue-grey
eyeshadow and mascara that did wonderful things to
her grey eyes, and a featherlight trace of rose-red
lipstick. She had caught her hair up high on her head
in a swinging ponytail, feminine but efficient. Nothing,
she determined, was going to interfere with her game
tonight. She meant to prove to Rupert, and anybody
who might have doubts, that she would make him a
worthy partner.

The car park at the club was nearly full. There was
obviously a good attendance for the try-out matches.
There were a couple of spaces free at the furthest point
from the clubhouse. Toni had just backed into one of
them when Rupert Devenish arrived in his elegant
dark blue Rover saloon and manoeuvred effortlessly
into the last space.

To Toni, keyed-up to prove herself on the court, it
seemed that he was already testing her, though this
was nonsense—he'd only just arrived and hadn't seen
her jostling for position. But she couldn't help recalling
that his offer to partner her at tennis had at least partly
come about because he had responded to her mute
call for help when Kieron's arm about her shoulder
had seemed a threat. She had been a good player, as
Bridget and others confirmed, but he had never seen
her play. Why should he accept other people's generous praise for her ability?

Her newly found confidence in herself, as a person
and as a tennis player, began to drain away. In a
sudden panic she decided she couldn't face him, or
anybody else for that matter. It had been ridiculous to
think that the initial meeting she had had with him

could have a lasting efect. He had boosted her morale briefly, and she was grateful to him for that. Perhaps it was a step forward, even though she was now about to take a partial step backwards.

'Hi,' he said, crossing from his car to hers, and opening her door as he spoke. 'Here, let me give you a hand.'

Tonguetied, Toni allowed him to put a hand beneath her elbow and support her as she jumped easily down from the high seat. It was such a natural, easy gesture on his part that she felt none of the unease such as she had experienced when Kieron had touched her. In fact, she enjoyed the feeling of Rupert's hand on her arm.

She felt her cheeks going red, and turned away to reach for her tote bag on the passenger-seat.

'I was afraid it might rain before we'd even had a chance to knock up,' he said, as she straightened and made herself meet his eyes. He moved a pace closer and took the bag from her nerveless fingers. 'You look marvellous—so cool, so indomitable. I'm relieved that you're my partner and not one of the opposition.' His voice was low, gravelly, intimate even, but his deep blue eyes looked into hers with a friendly frank gaze and a humorous twinkle, dispelling any sexual over-tones that she might have imagined were there.

'Yes, I thought too that it might rain.' She wondered if he had noticed her breathlessness.

Rupert had. Poor girl, he thought, she's still finding it an ordeal meeting people socially. He squeezed her arm gently.

'Come on,' he said, 'I'm the new boy, and I need your support. Let's give the opposition a run for their money.'

They walked side by side to the clubhouse.

The rain began to fall about forty minutes later, great blobs of moisture that soon fused together into sheets of water, so that by the time they had picked up their rackets and balls both Toni and Rupert and their opponents were soaked. This time they ran hand in hand back to the pavilion.

'Antonia, put this round you,' suggested Rupert, handing her his dry, thick cable-knit sweater, which he had left draped over a chair on the terrace.

Toni, about to refuse, not minding her wet clothes because she was so hot, looked down at herself and realised that her cotton shirt was clinging to her small breasts, making them look almost naked.

She felt her cheeks turn crimson with embarrassment. 'Thanks,' she mumbled, and grabbed at his sweater.

Rupert took the sleeves from her shaking hands and tied them into a loose knot, so that they draped down over her chest. 'It's all right,' he whispered softly. 'No one noticed.'

Except you, Toni thought, avoiding his eyes.

Someone put a tall, frosted glass in front of her. It was Kieron, a smiling Kieron.

'Non-alcoholic lager and lime,' he said, and added quietly, 'Sorry about last night—it wasn't fair to take it out on you for what happened. I'm sorry we're not playing together, but I'm partnering the gorgeous Melanie. So who's a lucky boy, then?'

Somehow Toni gathered her wits together. Rupert was quite right, nobody but he seemed to have noticed her wet shirt clinging to her bra-less bosom. She almost giggled at the expression that had sprung to mind, but instead turned a calm face towards Kieron.

'You are, Kieron—no contest.' She looked across the table to where Melanie was sitting in animated conversation with Terry Banks. 'We must have been blind at school, not realising that old String Bean was a caterpillar waiting to turn into a beautiful butterfly.'

'Yes,' said Kieron, his voice irritatingly complacent.

'And look who's netted her.' He looked away, then back at Toni, almost shyly. 'Funny thing is, I hadn't noticed since I came back here how different she looked, not until this morning really, when she phoned and asked me to be her partner in the mixed doubles. Last night, I thought you were the most sensational-looking girl in the club. Not a bit as I remembered you before you went away nursing and I went to Newcastle Uni.'

He didn't seem to consider that his words might in any way offend Toni, and indeed they didn't. She was totally relieved to find that he was no longer upset by what had happened last evening.

'Did you also forget what a good player Melanie is?' she said. 'Anyone who meets up with you two is going to have a tough match on their hands.'

'Yep, Melanie's great, and being so tall and slim she's got a tremendous reach, almost as good as mine and a match for nearly all the other chaps.'

He glanced across the table at Rupert, and grinned. 'Though not, I guess, a match for your boyfriend. He must be six foot two or three and pretty athletic with it, in spite of being—what?—thirty-fourish.'

Toni cringed inwardly at the expression boyfriend. For one thing, it wasn't true, and for another it didn't suit the thinly elegant doctor, with his shock of reddish-brown hair and high-bridged nose. Even now, in his rather sticky casual T-shirt, he looked distinguished. And, Toni reminded herself, he was a married man and not available to be anybody's boyfriend.

'I've no idea how old he is,' she replied stiffly. 'And he's *not* my boyfriend, whatever that silly expression means.'

'Still the high and mighty Miss King, aren't we?' said Kieron in a sarcastic but still good-humoured voice. 'Of course, you always were something of an ice maiden, but I thought life in a big city hospital might have changed all that.' He laughed, though not unkindly, and leaned towards her. 'I rather thought the ice might have been broken, or at least melted, with all those young medicos around.'

Toni sat quite still, her eyes on her drink, her hands clasped tightly round the glass. She knew Kieron's remark was quite innocent of intent to hurt or distress her. It was just a silly sort of comment made by a young man who probably thought himself more sophisticated than his local contemporaries. But his words did hurt, none the less.

Ice maiden—that was what Patrick had called her that night before. . .

She pushed her chair back from the table with a loud scrape. 'I'm going home,' she said brightly, not looking at anyone in particular, and especially avoiding Rupert's eye. 'It doesn't look as if it's going to stop raining, and the light's bad, so we won't get any more play in tonight. See you—goodnight.' She gave what she hoped was a nonchalant wave and strode off.

Kieron said loudly to her retreating back, 'Look here, I say. . .' but Toni pretended not to hear.

Somehow she got herself out of the room. Surely everybody was looking at her? There was no one behind the desk in reception. She paused for a moment, looking out through the glass doors at the streaming rain. She would make a dash for it. Automatically her hand went to her side where her bag should be hanging, to fish out her car keys. It wasn't there. Of course, it was on the floor by her chair in the bar.

'Oh, no!' The muted cry was wrenched from her. She couldn't go back into that room, face all those people again, make some feeble excuse for rushing away. She leaned against the door, and with difficulty held back a sob. To think that this day, which had begun to happily, had deteriorated to this. In silent fury, she banged her fists on the plate glass.

A strong, lean hand, as brown as her own, closed over her clenched fists.

'Don't,' said Rupert Devenish. 'You'll hurt yourself.'

Toni turned a ravaged face towards him. 'It doesn't matter,' she mumbled. 'This was all a mistake.' She pulled one hand from his restraining grip and waved it comprehensively around, indicating the terrace and courts beyond. 'It was silly to think I could slip back as if nothing had happened.'

'Does anybody who matters think you should return as if nothing had happened?'

Toni stared at him. 'What do you mean?' she demanded, and then, truculently, 'Do you know what happened, do you know why I haven't been out and about for yonks?'

'No, I don't know exactly, I can only make an educated guess that you've been badly hurt. How, when, where and why, I don't know. But, Antonia, my dear, old friends, real friends, who do know these things, wouldn't expect you to integrate at once. They would do, as I'm sure they already have done, everything they could to help you get sorted out, but they wouldn't expect miracles. Perhaps you expected a miracle and have been disappointed.'

There was no condemnation in his voice, only understanding. But he was right, of course—she had expected a miracle of sorts since he had arrived on the scene. Not that she could tell him this, in spite of the close, almost spiritual connection she felt for and with him. Maybe it was all in her own mind, maybe she had misinterpreted his reaction to her. Perhaps all that had passed between them then had been a joke, a mistake, and she had made it something special. Perhaps the eye contact in the hothouse two days ago, and repeated in the surgery later, had only been significant to her.

'I want to go home,' she said stonily, 'but I've left my bag with my keys in in the bar.'

'I've got it here, Antonia—don't worry, I'll see you home and we'll sort things out.'

Mutely she reached for her bag and he handed it to her. She rummaged around in it until she found her car keys.

'Thank you,' she said in a voice that she knew sounded cold and unfriendly. 'But there's no need for you to trouble yourself. Please go back to the others.' As she started to push open the door, she turned to face him. 'Sorry about the match. I think we'd have done pretty well as a team, but I'm sure they'll fix you up with someone else.'

Rupert looked at first surprised and then irritated. He said impatiently, sarcastically, 'Well, I thought better of you than that. What the hell are you talking about, a new partner—you're surely not going to back out now, are you? You've got more guts than that. Now that you've taken the plunge, for God's sake stick it out.'

His angry words were like a slap in the face, and the tears she had been fighting back threatened to burst forth. He had said what she would have expected from almost anyone else, but not from him. Other people might, in their ignorance, talk about pulling oneself together, but not Dr Devenish. He was different— well, she'd thought he was different.

So much for all her fantasising about his strength and rock-like qualities. When it came down to it, he was just a man like any other, intent on getting his own way and not having his plans upset. He didn't want to have to find another tennis partner. The idea was enough to change him from being sympathetic to aggressive.

Her chest and head hurt from holding back the tears, but she was damned if she would let him see her cry. Keys at the ready in one hand, she flung the heavy glass door open with the other and dashed towards the Land Rover. Even prepared as she was, she was still fumbling to get the slippery wet key into the lock, when Rupert appeared beside her.

He took the bunch of keys from her shaking fingers and dropped them back into her bag, then took her arm firmly just above the elbow.

'No.' She stared at him through the pouring rain. It was streaming down his face, and his thick reddish-brown hair was plastered against his head like a helmet. Toni could feel tendrils of her own hair which had escaped from her ponytail pasting themselves against her face. Water ran into her eyes, and she blinked. It ran into her mouth, and she licked her lips. The rainwater tasted salty. She realised then that she was crying as she hadn't cried since she was a child, with great heaving, painful sobs that hurt her chest.

'That's better,' said the doctor softly, and smiled at her, his deep blue eyes inky dark with compassion and understanding. Somehow, through her dreadful pain and despair, she knew he wasn't angry or aggressive, and never had been. He had wanted her to cry. He had deliberately given her a shock to make her cry. In a muddled way she perceived that tears were a treatment, and he had prescribed them.

'Here.' He opened the door of his car and pushed her gently inside. She sank on to the sumptuous leather, head bowed, tears running between her fingers as she pressed her hands to her face in a hopeless attempt to hide them.

She felt Rupert sit down in the driver's seat beside her, and a towel being patted over her head and neck, then his arms were about her shoulders as he drew her

to him. Still the tears raged in a torrent, and she kept
her hands over her face.

'That's right, love, just let it go,' he whispered,
rocking her in his arms as if she were a child. He
pulled a rug from the back seat and wrapped it round
her.

How long she had sobbed and snivelled against his
already wet shirt, she had no idea. When at last she
surfaced, and pulled a little away from him, he had a
large plain handkerchief at the ready.

'Here—blow,' he said in a matter-of-fact voice, and
engulfed her small nose in white linen. She blew
noisily, gulped, took the hanky from him and blew her
nose again.

'Thanks,' she said, and then in a thread of a voice,
'Oh, gosh, I'm so t-tired.' She felt herself slipping
down in the seat, and struggled to sit up. 'I'm s-sorry—
so r-rude.' She couldn't keep her eyes open, or do
anything about her stammer. She ought to be embarrassed for having given way and cried like a baby for
what seemed like hours, but she didn't; all she felt was
empty, absolutely empty, and exhausted, totally
exhausted.

She tried to push away the rug and feel for the door
handle. 'M-must get home,' she mumbled.

Rupert reached over and fastened her seatbelt and
locked the car door. 'You're not fit to drive, Antonia,'
he explained patiently. 'I'll take you home. Something
can be arranged about picking up the Land Rover
tomorrow. Now go to sleep. I'll wake you up when I
get you home.'

Toni felt she should protest. Grandpa would worry
if she arrived home like this, she ought to. . . Ought
to what?

'I'll explain everything,' said Rupert quietly. He
gave her a reassuring smile that she could just make
out in the fading light. 'Don't worry now, everything's

going to be all right.' He tucked the rug round her once again and patted her shoulder in an impersonal, professional manner. 'You've needed to cry like that for a long time. Doesn't do to bottle things up, but it's an exhausting business, dealing with one's emotions—traumatic.'

He looked gravely across at her as he switched on the engine. His narrow, intelligent face and deep set eyes conveyed the same sense of utter integrity and reliability, as they had a few days before, when she had first met him. How could she ever have doubted him, even for a minute?

She was only just conscious of being driven home and of responding in a vague detached manner to her grandfather and Mrs Klemp when the doctor deposited her on the doorstep.

There was a murmur of voices and she muttered a goodnight and a thank-you to Rupert, as Mrs Klemp guided her up the wide oak staircase.

Looking down from the balustraded gallery into the dimly lit hall below, she saw Rupert and her grandfather disappear into the small sitting-room.

She went to sleep with the picture in her mind of the doctor giving an arm to her grandfather as they left the hall. It was a comforting picture and seemed a fitting end to a peculiar day.

CHAPTER SEVEN

Toni, who for years had woken automatically at six-thirty, slept on the following morning. When she woke, it was to find Mrs Klemp in her room, pulling back the curtains, flooding the room with brilliant sunshine. It was eleven o'clock. The marvellous aroma of fried bacon and fresh coffee filled the air. Her nostrils twitched with pleasure.

'Gosh, I'm starving!' she said, and then realised with a jolt that it must be late, because the sun was high in the sky. And what on earth was Mrs Klemp doing here? She sat up and stared at the laden tray set on the table beside her bed. 'What the hell's all this about?' she asked.

'Doctor's orders—Dr Devenish's orders before he left last night. You were to sleep the clock round and have your breakfast in bed. And he was quite right too. You look tons better this morning—a new woman. Now come on, young lady, get that into you, and no nonsense about muesli and such. A good old-fashioned breakfast won't hurt you for once.'

Memory of the previous evening and all that had happened came flooding back. Toni felt her cheeks go red and then pale as she recalled her reaction to Kieron's innocent though unkind remark, and her precipitate flight from the tennis club. And then the tears, buckets of them, mostly shed all over the already wet Rupert Devenish. What must he have thought of her, however kindly he had treated her at the time? He must have wondered—still wondered, probably— if she was crackers.

I feel such a fool, food would choke me, she thought.

She gazed at the delicious rashers of bacon, the butter-browned mushrooms, the perfect sunny-side-up egg and crimson halves of the grilled tomatoes. Her mouth watered, but she set it in an obstinate line, ridiculously determined to punish herself for the previous evening's fiasco.

Mrs Klemp was standing by the bed, smiling at her encouragingly. 'Go on, love, eat it up. The doctor said you were to have a good breakfast. He was so kind, and that concerned about you when he brought you home.'

'He was pretty free with his orders last night, wasn't he?' Toni didn't mean to be rude and ungrateful, but she couldn't make up her mind whether to be pleased or angry with him, ordering her to do this or do that. He sounded as if he really cared. Mrs Klemp obviously thought he did, and already seemed to be his willing slave. His word was law as far as she was concerned.

Toni suddenly realised how childishly she was behaving. It was worrying Mrs Klemp, who was looking quite bothered.

'Take no notice of me,' she said to that good lady. 'I'm just being dog-in-the-mangerish. This is smashing, just what the doctor ordered.' They both laughed at her unintended pun. 'And I am ravenous.' She polished off the egg and bacon and a load of toast and marmalade in short order, and drained the coffee-pot dry.

'Well, I'm glad to see you enjoyed it. The doctor will be pleased.'

'The doctor,' replied Toni in a tart voice, 'will never know whether I ate breakfast or not.'

'Oh, but he will, my dear—he's calling in later today to see how you are, and he said he'd ask especially.'

'Well, of all the cheek, checking up on me like that.'

Toni felt compelled to object to Rupert's actions, but it wasn't an honest reaction, she admitted to herself. She was glad he was showing such concern for her, glad he was coming to see her today, in spite of feeling some embarrassment at having to face him after the events of last night.

It was afternoon before he arrived, and she had almost given up hope of his coming. In fact, she was so busy potting up that for the first time in hours she had ceased to think about him. So his arrival was a shock.

He came in through the door from the seed house, and the first she knew of his presence was when he stood at her elbow and said, 'Hi,' in a deep but quiet voice.

Toni dropped the small plastic pot containing a two-inch-high cistus that she had just transplanted from a box of seedlings.

'I'm so sorry,' said the doctor, bending as she did to pick up the tiny plant. His gentian-blue eyes peered into hers as they crouched beneath the bench. 'I'm so sorry,' he repeated. 'I didn't mean to startle you.' He looked down at the spilled soil and battered leaves. 'Will it be all right?' he asked, genuine concern in his voice, and then, 'What is it?'

Toni recovered from the pleasant shock of finding him by her side, though her stammer was bothersome. She smiled. 'Oh, I-I th-think so, it'll be all right. It's a rock rose, and they're remarkably t-tough, rather like babies really, you know, h-half dead one moment and b-begging for food the next.'

'Ah, food.' He too smiled. 'Did you eat the gargantuan breakfast that I've no doubt Mrs Klemp presented you with?'

'W-well, it was doctor's orders, and I wouldn't dream of disobeying.' Toni was delighted that the whole sentence came out loaded with sarcasm but with hardly a double-take.

Rupert gave a deep, throaty laugh. 'You're incorrigible,' he said, and leaned over and kissed the tip of her nose, 'and delightful.' Even as he did it he offered a silent prayer that he hadn't scared her off. Sometimes it was difficult to equate this bright, fearless-looking young woman with the frightened, probably abused female who hid beneath the cool façade. But he knew he must tread warily if he was to win her confidence and, he hoped, at some future date, her love, and keep it.

She busied herself with pots and plants and tried not to think that his kiss was important. She remembered that he had wanted a plant for someone in hospital.

'By the way, do you still want that plant—you know, a scented one for someone in hospital, but something that would stand the heat of a ward? You were very specific about it.'

'Yes, please. I can deliver it on my way up to town.' His eyebrows arched up into triangles over his incredibly blue eyes, elongating his face even more than usual, emphasising his intelligence, his male sexiness. 'Have you got anything—well, for want of a better word, sophisticated, rather understated, cool-looking?'

Heavens, Toni thought, I wonder what this lady is like? Surely it had to be a lady. 'Yes, just the thing. I thought about it after you enquired the other day, and a fragrant-leafed pelargonium would be admirable.'

'A geranium?' Rupert frowned.

Toni laughed, feeling all at once confident, knowing rather more about plants than the doctor did.

'They're not all simply crimson and rather gaudy, though I personally think the gaudy reds have a lot to offer, but for a more *sophisticated* bloom, one has to go a long way to beat citriodorum, a citrus-scented

geranium with a virginal white bloom. Grows to about
two feet, but beautiful and elegant, and what I'd call
user-friendly. That is, it needs regular watering but
will manage if forgotten.'

Rupert smiled, a tolerant, kindly smile. 'That sounds
just right for Sophie,' he said softly, lovingly. 'Right,
Antonia, you've made yourself a sale. From where do
I collect this, pelargonium of virtue?'

Toni giggled. 'Very good, I've got some in the
frames outside, temperate warmth, but they can stand
heat.'

They went together to choose a plant.

'Rub your thumb and forefinger gently over a leaf,'
advised Toni. 'The scent is delightful.'

'Well, so it is,' said Rupert, obviously surprised.
'Sophie will love this.'

'Do you want a card to go with it?'

'Why not? In case I can't see her—I'm rather short
of time.'

She gave him a card. He wrote on it: 'Darling
Sophie, looking forward to having you and new
addition home. All my love, Rupert'.

He handed it to Toni to attach to the plant. She
stared at him for a moment in stunned silence, then
gathered her wits and began tying the card to the
plant. Of course, that was why nobody had seen or
heard anything of a Mrs Devenish—she was obviously
in hospital giving birth to their umpteenth baby. There
simply had to be several more, or even the cool Dr
Devenish would have been behaving rather more like
an expectant father. He certainly wouldn't have said
casually that he might not have time to visit his wife.

She fumbled with the tie. Rupert took it from her
and with steady fingers fixed it to the plant, giving
Toni a questioning sideways glance as he did so.

'I d-didn't realise it was for a m-mother and baby,'

she explained. 'We do special cards for the occasion.
Would you prefer one of those?'

'No, thanks—it sounds revolting. Sophie wouldn't
appreciate it at all. She's a very beautiful, rather aloof
sort of woman.' He smiled down at Toni to take the
sting out of his words. 'I'm sorry, I don't mean to be
rude, I'm sure your special cards are fine for some
people, but not, I assure you, for Sophie.'

Although he was nice about refusing, Toni felt she
had made an awful gaffe to even suggest a special card.
Not that it mattered. If he was the sort of man who
went around kissing other women when his wife had
just produced a new baby, a mild social gaffe was as
nothing.

'Hell!' he said, suddenly looking at his watch. 'I've
got to be off, I'm afraid. I'll be up in town until
tomorrow afternoon, but I'll be back in time for our
match in the evening—weather, of course, permitting.
See you then, Antonia.' He took her hand and bent
his head down. She thought he was about to kiss her
again, and took a step backward. She didn't know
what rules he played by, but they weren't the same as
hers. No way was she going to cheat on his wife and
new baby, even if the doctor and perhaps the elegant
Sophie found it acceptable.

He let go of her hand at once and smiled at her in a
friendly fashion. But a wave of disappointment washed
over him. The way that she had recoiled from his
touch seemed to take him back to square one again,
just as he thought he was making progress. It was odd,
since she appeared to have accepted the fleeting kiss
that he had planted on her nose with pleasure. Last
night had been, he was sure, a crisis point, which he
had hoped might be a springboard to a return to
normal for this lovely girl with whom he had fallen
head over heels in love.

With all his heart he wished he didn't have to go up

to London to his teaching hospital, but he was booked
for several lectures that in all conscience he couldn't
avoid. And of course, he must call in at the Devon-
Spencer Clinic, to see—or leave a message for—
Sophie and deliver the plant. Thank God he had seen
the baby, both when it was born and a few days after.
He really couldn't be expected to do more. His mother
visited the clinic daily, and soon Sophie and the baby
would be back in the bosom of the family, and he
would do his damnedest to help out.

He put the plant carefully in the car on the passenger-seat and climbed in beside it.

'Goodbye,' he said to Toni. 'Take care.' He moved
off down the drive with a spurt of gravel. For once he
avoided looking for her image in the mirror. He
couldn't bear the thought of leaving her looking for-
lorn and friendless; it hurt too much.

Resolutely, Toni returned to work. 'I will not,' she
told herself, 'let the two-timing Dr Devenish throw
me.' But the idea that he was two-timing hurt. Of all
people, she wanted him to be whiter than white—
flawless. It was a silly idea, of course; people weren't
like that, black or white, good or bad.

She mulled over what he had said and done since
she had met him only days before. From their first
meeting he had made no secret of the fact that he had
a family, and he'd been friendly then, but in a rather
avuncular fashion. Even the eye-to-eye contact she'd
had with him, though riveting and full of meaning, had
not seemed overtly sexual. All his other actions had
seemed protective and unthreatening, and last night
he had been wonderful. But today, seeing him write
an affectionate if rather cool message to his wife, only
minutes after he had kissed her teasingly on the nose,
changed everything.

Except, she reminded herself, nothing could alter

the fact that it was through him she had regained the confidence to return to the social round. She would always remain grateful to him for that.

As for dear old Dr Meredith, Uncle Morris as he once was, he seemed to think highly of Rupert Devenish, and he was supposed to know quite a lot about him. According to Bridget, Dr Meredith and Rupert's father had been great friends. Surely he wouldn't condone any loose behaviour from a colleague, a doctor whom he had introduced into the practice. There must be some explanation for Rupert's seeming indifference to his wife, and his willingness to look elsewhere for distraction.

Perhaps she was being over-sensitive about it. The thought cheered her somewhat.

'I must ask Dr Meredith,' she said out loud to the warm, throbbing glasshouse, 'what he knows about Rupert.'

The idea that Dr Meredith would not have engaged Rupert if there was anything in the least bit suspect about him was a great comfort, and Toni got through the rest of the afternoon in a reasonably hopeful state of mind.

It was just after six and she was tidying up for the night when the phone rang. Ironically, since she had thought on and off about him for much of the afternoon in connection with Rupert, it was Dr Meredith.

'Toni, I'm coming up tonight to give your grandfather a game of chess, but I'd like to have a word with you in private, before I see him. Do you think you might hover on the terrace at about half-past seven?'

'W-well, yes, of course. There's n-nothing wrong, seriously wrong, with Grandpa, is there?'

'No, my dear, this has nothing to do with him, at least not his health, but I want to put a proposition to you without him getting involved.' He sounded very cheerful.

'How intriguing, very cloak-and-dagger.'

Only after she put down the phone did Toni wonder if the proposition might have anything to do with Rupert, and, if it did, would it automatically answer some of the questions that were bothering her. At least tonight's meeting with the older doctor would give her an opportunity to seek out some information about his enigmatic partner.

After an early supper, she settled her grandfather in the small sitting-room, with the chess table at the ready and, on a side table, whisky, water and glasses. He was as always looking forward to a game with his old friend.

'I'll bring in sandwiches later, Grandpa,' Toni assured him. 'I'm going down to the village presently to see Mrs Deal. She wants some help filling in the insurance forms to do with Jack's accident.'

'You'll make sure she's all right, won't you—money and everything? We mustn't let her go short.'

'Of course, Grandpa. You are a darling.' And that was something I wouldn't have had the courage to say a week ago, Toni reflected.

The old man muttered gruffly, and Toni, with a smile, went out on to the terrace to wait for Dr Meredith.

He arrived promptly at seven-thirty.

'I'm bursting with curiosity,' said Toni. 'Please don't keep me in suspense. What on earth is this proposition?'

'How would you like to come and help out at the surgery two or three days a week?' he asked her, taking her at her word and not beating about the bush.

'W-work? At the surgery?'

'That's what I said, my dear. We're desperate for a

good clinic nurse. Mary Mates starts her maternity leave next week, and the nurse who was going to come as a temp has backed out at the last minute. I could go to the agency, but I'm not very happy about that, and when your name was suggested it seemed an ideal solution.'

'But Bridget knows I've got plenty to do here, and anyway, I don't want to go back to nursing—well, not yet. You know why—I'm not ready.'

'You never will be, Toni, if you don't take the plunge. You've made a start by returning to the tennis club. I can't tell how delighted I was to see you there the other night. You granny would have been pleased. And I believe she'd tell you that the time is right now to pick up the threads of your nursing again. You'll be among friends at the surgery. What could be better?'

'But I'm out of practice,' Toni protested. 'I'd be terrified that I'd let you down.'

'You rose beautifully to the occasion the other night when you came to the rescue of that poor child with the burns. And friend Devenish is full of admiration for the way you coped with Jack Deal's accident.'

Her face flamed at the mention of Rupert's name, and the compliment he had paid her. She turned away and idly dead-headed some of the roses that twined about the pillars of the terrace. Now would be the time to question Dr Meredith about his younger colleague, but somehow the words would not come.

'What exactly does your clinic nurse do?' she asked.

'Bloods, injections, ECGs, helps Pat MacNiece with the Well Woman clinic, cervical smears—that sort of thing. Nothing you can't handle. Come on, Toni, give it a try. Come down to the surgery tomorrow—any time, as long as you let Mary know, and suss it out.'

Just as the thought of Rupert Devenish being present at the tennis club had been the deciding factor in persuading her to put in an appearance, so now was the knowledge that if she worked at the surgery, she would see him virtually daily. Her earlier qualms blew away like mist before the wind.

'OK, Uncle Morris,' she heard herself say, unconsciously addressing him as she had when a child. 'I'll give it a try. That is, I'll go down to the surgery tomorrow and talk to Mary.'

The doctor, who she suddenly realised had aged since her grandmother's death, kissed her on both cheeks.

'You'll make me a very happy man if you join us,' he said softly. 'And keep up the "Uncle" bit. I thought you'd given me the brush-off a long time ago. It's nice to be family again.'

He marched off along the terrace and went into the small sitting-room. She heard him greet her grandfather and waited for a moment listening to the rumble of their voices, before leaving by way of the rose garden to drive down to the village and her appointment with Mrs Deal.

The following morning she woke with the feeling that something tremendous was going to happen, and then she remembered what it was. Her tummy churned with a mixture of fear, excitement and incredulity. Had she really promised Uncle Morris she would consider the nursing job? Yes, she had, and the sooner she got cracking down in the nursery to get some work done there, the better.

From the purely growing part of the job, things were beginning to ease off in the hothouses. Once the current batch of seeds was transferred for potting up, the slack season would be upon her. Routine cleaning of the sheds would commence as each of them was emptied of current stock. Not until the autumn, when seeds were sown for spring plants and the Christmas trees and other seasonal plants prepared for sale, would the nursery need full-time attention.

If she was going to start nursing again, now would be an ideal time. She could fit in another job very neatly with her nursery work.

Bridget was the first person she met when she arrived at the Health Centre.

She was her usual bubbly self. 'I say, this is great, Toni, you coming to work here. I couldn't believe my ears when Mary told me you were going to relieve her while she's away.'

'But you suggested me to Dr Meredith.'

'No, I didn't, but I wish I'd thought of it. Now that you're beginning to return to the land of the living, nothing could be better.'

'But he said. . .' What in fact had Dr Meredith said? That her name had been suggested, not who had suggested it. She had assumed that it was Bridget and he hadn't corrected her assumption, but neither had he confirmed it. So if not Bridget, who? Could it have been. . .? In her bones she knew it was Rupert Devenish.

Dr Meredith came out of his office. 'Ah, Toni, there you are—come on, I've got a minute, let's go through and see Mary.'

Directly they were in the corridor leading to the various offices and treatment-rooms, Toni rounded on the doctor.

'I know it wasn't Bridget who suggested me for the job, so who was it?' she demanded.

'My dear girl, I think you've already made a guess at that, haven't you?'

'It was Dr Devenish.'

'Yes, and I didn't disabuse you about its being Bridget, because I thought you were more likely to consider the proposition if the idea came from an old friend, rather than a new acquaintance.'

Toni, always fair, conceded this. 'Yes, I expect you're right. B-but I don't understand why he should have thought of m-me. After all, he doesn't know me very w-well.' She was furious with herself for stammering. 'He hasn't known me long enough, and he knows nothing of my nursing ability, except in an emergency.'

'Perhaps knowing someone doesn't depend on time as we choose to think of it,' said the doctor gently. 'Just as age has little to do with what one person feels for another.'

Toni knew he was referring then to her grandmother and his love for her. Last night, when she noted how he had aged recently, she had understood properly for the first time how hard it must be for him to pretend to be just an old friend of the family. But why was he making a parallel between his situation and Rupert Devenish's proposal that she resume her nursing? It was almost as if he was suggesting that there might be more to Rupert's suggestion than just professional interest. Could it be that, and would he convey such a possibility if he had any doubts about his younger colleague's credentials?

A dozen questions rushed through Toni's mind, but before she could voice any of them Mary Mates, showing a patient out of the treatment-room, called to her.

'Toni, this is marvellous. When our dear Dr Meredith here,' she touched the doctor's arm affectionately, 'suggested you taking over, I was thrilled. There's no one I'd rather looked after my patients. After all, we trained at the same place, and we've lived here since forever. It seems just so right that you should keep things ticking over while I'm away.'

Her exuberance, and the certainty with which she

assumed that Toni was definitely going to replace her, was breathtaking.

Dr Meredith sensed this. 'Look,' he said hastily, 'I'll leave you two ladies to it, to work something out. When you've finished, Toni, come and see me in my office.' He turned and all but ran down the corridor.

'Coward,' Mary called after him in a teasing voice. He lifted his hand in acknowledgement, but continued on his way.

'What was all that about?' asked Toni.

'He's so keen for you to come, and so worried that you won't. It's made him edgy, quite different from his usual calm self.'

'I'll say. I've never seen him like this. But you do know, Mary, that I'm only here to test the waters, as it were. I haven't agreed definitely to come.'

'Of course I understand, but I think you're going to take to this like a duck to water. Working here will be right up your street.

Mary was right. Toni loved being back in harness. She had meant to simply look and listen, but in fact spent the rest of the morning helping with taking bloods, and labelling specimen bottles for despatch to the hospital laboratory at twelve-thirty. Except in a dire emergency, this was the drill.

Showing Toni the day-book, Mary explained, 'This is why I try to get all blood and urine or other samples that have to be sent to the lab done in the morning. It means checking against appointments made by patients at any time the previous day, and fitting in patients who may be referred during the morning clinics. And occasionally the doctors will bring in specimens from their visits, so it's important to check each of them when they come back from their rounds. They don't always remember to tell you, and then you're left with specimens which you have to deliver to the hospital yourself.'

'Doctors!' said Toni, and the two nurses raised their eyebrows at each other.

By late afternoon, Toni had syringed four sets of ears, given three hay-fever injections, removed stitches from two patients, one with a healed leg wound, the other with a hand injury, and reassured a small child that taking a throat swab was fun, and not to be gagged at.

When at last she went home, she was tired, elated, and full of joy at being back in the nursing swing. She had agreed to take over from Mary for four days a week, as from the following week, and was looking forward to it with a gut feeling of happiness. This was right, this was what she was meant to be doing. Nursing was her life.

She showered and changed into her tennis gear ready for the match and her encounter with Rupert, feeling whole, complete, for the first time in ages.

Before she left, she visited her grandfather and told him of her plans to return to nursing via the surgery.

The brigadier was quietly pleased and philosophical.

'Yes,' he said, 'Morris told me last night that you might be going to help him out. Duty, my dear, that's the name of the game.'

Toni couldn't suppress a giggle. 'Well,' she said, 'at the moment, the name of the game is tennis. I'm off to slaughter them, Grandpa, or rather Rupert Devenish and I are going to slaughter them between us.' She realised she had said Rupert's name without a tremor. That must be a good sign.

'Ah, yes, Devenish—Morris reminded me that I knew his father, young medical chap doing his service in India. He seems to have sorted out this damned ulcer, it feels all right.'

'Oh, good,' said Toni, rather stunned by this revelation. 'I'll tell him tonight when I see him, I'm sure he'll be pleased to know that his treatment is working.'

Rupert was already at the tennis club when Toni arrived.

'Hi,' he said in his deep voice. 'I hear we're going to be partners at work as well as at play.'

His words took her breath away. She had been wondering how to tackle him about the part he had played in her getting the nursing job.

'Yes,' she agreed lamely. 'I'm starting officially at the surgery next week.'

'I'm so glad,' he said, and his gentian-blue eyes bored into hers. 'I hate to see talent wasted, and you're a born nurse.'

'Seedlings need nursing too,' she said, trying to sound triumphant. It was true, but would he believe it?

'Yes, of course they do, and so do people. You're good at both.' He put a hand on her bare arm, making her shiver. 'It's going to be lovely having you in the surgery. I think we should have a drink to celebrate the occasion.'

Toni realised they were in effect celebrating her return to the world, however small and intimate, of Peckhurst and her home village of Washbourne.

'Cheers,' they said to each other as they clinked their glasses of champagne spritzers.

Rupert added, 'To a long and very happy partnership, Antonia,' and his blue eyes met her grey ones over the rims of their tall, frosted glasses. 'Now, let's go and demolish the opposition.'

They walked out from the shady terrace into the blue and gold of a perfect summer's evening.

'By the way,' said Rupert as they were parking their spare rackets and balls on the seat at the side of their court, 'the plant was a great success with my sister-in-law—she loved it.'

For a moment Toni thought she was going to faint with shock. Sophie wasn't his wife! The cool, elegant Sophie was his sister-in-law. He wasn't two-timing anyone, he was the honourable man that she wanted him to be. Far from being an indifferent husband, he was a caring brother-in-law.

'Oh, good,' she murmured.

She thought, what about the ring, the wedding ring that she had seen at their first meeting? If Sophie wasn't. . .? She recalled the sun sparkling on Rupert's gold cufflinks, and his watch, and the wide band on his ring finger. She stared down at his hands. No ring on his left hand—his watch was there, slim and elegant on his bare brown wrist, but definitely *no ring*.

She blurted out, 'Your,' she had the sense to say, '*signet ring*—wasn't it on your other hand? I've just noticed.' She bent down and made a great thing of tying her laces.

Rupert followed her gaze, and frowned. He was only mildly surprised by her sudden interest in his ring. He raised his right hand, where a handsome, wide platinum-gold signet ring encircled a finger. 'I had a wasp sting,' he explained, 'and my finger swelled, so I put my ring on my other hand. It's better now, and I've switched it back.'

Toni took several deep uneven breaths, not even caring if he noticed. 'Oh, I am glad,' she said in a voice trembling with happiness, 'so very glad.' If she was too enthusiastic because Sophie liked the plant she had chosen for her, or because he had recovered from the wasp sting, she didn't care. Cheerfully she said, 'Come on, partner, let's beat them hollow.'

Rupert smiled down at her, his blue eyes dark with love, a love he knew he must keep hidden from her until he had her wholehearted trust. He wasn't sure what had caused her sudden burst of joy, but he was only too pleased to share it with her.

'Oh, we'll do that,' he said.

They did. Six-two, four-six, six love.

CHAPTER EIGHT

FROM day one, Toni was thrown in at the deep end at the surgery. The local holiday camp, receiving a new influx of visitors on the Saturday, had by Monday produced a dozen or more cases of food poisoning. It was a mild attack. Two people were sent to hospital, but most were treated at the camp in the well arranged sanatorium.

The doctors at the Health Centre, who by arrangement accepted holidaymakers as temporary residents, were fully involved. Since the most ill patients had been transferred to hospital, the drill for the others was high fluid intake and rest and warmth until the symptoms subsided, and, in a few cases, an anti-emetic to treat excessive reflex vomiting.

One or two holidaymakers had presented themselves at the surgery early on Monday morning with obvious symptoms of food poisoning, but it was only later in the morning that the full picture emerged.

Toni had just finished taking blood samples from patients already booked in by Mary previously, when Rupert came to the clinic-room door.

'Nurse King,' he sounded very formal—probably, thought Toni, because her last patient was still within earshot, 'please pack a bag with some syringes and two of each of these anti-emetics that I've listed, and meet me in the car park in,' he consulted his watch, 'say ten minutes. I've cleared it with Dr Meredith, and we're going up to the holiday camp—several cases of food posioning there. I'll explain more as we go.'

'Yes, of course, Doctor.' Her reply sounded stilted, but then so had his request. Toni smiled to herself as she got the bag ready; it seemed odd being so formal with Rupert. No doubt it would be more relaxed on the drive to the holiday camp.

But it wasn't. Rupert was already in the car when she joined him. He looked detached and deep in thought as he leaned over and pushed the door open so she could get in to the passenger-seat.

'Got everything?' he asked.

'Everything you asked for, plus sterile swabs and specimen cartons. I wasn't sure you'd need them, but it seems a possibility.'

He looked marginally less distant. 'Yes—fine, good thinking.'

There was a trained nurse and several helpers at the sanatorium. It really was a well run camp, and it was difficult to believe that negligence had caused the problem.

'But that's something that the powers that be will have to decide,' Rupert had explained on the drive there. 'All food-poisoning cases have to be reported these days. We just do what we can and hand over to the experts to find out the cause.'

The senior nurse had saved some specimens of vomit, and had written out a list of food that each patient had taken over the last twenty-four hours.

'That's very competent of you, Sister,' Rupert praised the middle-aged nurse in charge, sounding his usual warm, friendly self. 'As far as I can see, you're doing everything that can be done to contain the situation—plenty of fluids, rest and warmth. And you have the usual range of painkillers available, which of course you may give as necessary within the maximum dose. Please contact the surgery if anything extra is needed. Fortunately, except for those two who had to be admitted to hospital, it seems to be a mild attack, but each case must be reported, as I'm sure you know.'

He gave the nurse one of his nicest smiles, and she

responded as any normal female would to his charm, falling over herself to confirm that she would do everything he asked.

Toni had been pleased she was accompanying Rupert to the camp, but somewhat disconcerted to find that he continued to be so distant with her. The little conversation they had had since they left the surgery had seemed formal and coolly professional. He wasn't exactly unfriendly, but there was no warmth in his manner. At the camp he addressed her as 'Nurse' quite sharply, in one instance causing her to fumble when she was drawing up an intramuscular injection of promethazine for one lady who was being particularly sick.

She pulled herself together, determined not to be put off by his manner, persuading herself that this might be his working persona. After all, he was a very senior physician, and this was the first time she had worked with him professionally. The other occasions had been emergencies and she had been acting in a voluntary guise. Perhaps he felt the need to stress his position as doctor with her as nurse as a reminder that their friendliness on the tennis court should not be brought to work.

No, this couldn't be true. He knew she wouldn't take advantage of their friendship when working, and, anyway, he was equally friendly with Bridget and other staff at the Health Centre when off duty, and it didn't appear to make him less friendly when they were working. Quite the reverse, from all that she'd heard. Rupert was universally liked by his colleagues in all the departments, and his sociability was one of the qualities most admired in the short while he had been at the Health Centre.

Toni's mind was in turmoil as they drove back in silence. What an uncomfortable first morning. She glanced sideways at Rupert. His profile looked stern, unyielding. There was a mark on the bridge of his nose where his half-spectacles had rested when he'd put them on to write up prescriptions, reminding her of the occasion when he had put on his specs to write up her grandfather's treatment, in the hothouse at the nursery. It showed slightly pale against his tan. For some reason she found it rather endearing, a small flaw on his otherwise near-perfect features.

They drew up in the car park, and to her surprise, before she could stir from her seat, Rupert turned to face her and put out a tentative hand. 'Wait, please.' She turned to face him. He no longer looked stern or withdrawn, and, though he wasn't smiling, his mobile mouth quirked slightly at the corners in a sardonic fashion, as if he might be smiling inwardly. She met his eyes, and was quite shocked by their violet depths. They were concealing something—could it be pain, distress?

'Rupert, are you all right? You look. . .' She didn't know how to finish. For the tiniest moment she felt a *frisson* of fear tinged with excitement trickle over her. It was gone almost before she was aware of her reaction to his piercing scrutiny. She repeated, 'Are you all right?'

He smiled at her then, a normal smile, his nice, rather wide mouth opening to reveal large, even white teeth. His eyes lost their inky depths, resuming their more normal gentian-blue colour. He was, in fact, back to normal.

'I'm fine,' he answered to her anxious enquiry. 'Sorry if I was a bit offhand back at the camp—I was trying to come to terms with something. I shouldn't have let it interfere with work, or our relationship, on duty or off. It won't happen again, promise.' He touched her cheek, briefly, a feather-light touch, from which he quickly drew back.

The intimacy of the gesture both disturbed and

pleased her. She put up her own hand to touch the spot where his had rested momentarily.

'Am I forgiven?' he asked.

'Yes, of course—not that there's anything to forgive. I hadn't noticed anything particularly unusual in your attitude.'

'You're a rotten liar, Antonia King,' he said, sounding amused. 'But thanks anyway. Friends?' He held out his hand, and Toni put hers into it.

Solemnly, sitting in his car in the hot, dusty concourse of the Health Centre car park, they shook hands, sealing a pact of friendship that held strange undercurrents of emotion for them both.

They got out of the car, Rupert coming round to open the door before she had a chance to do so. Side by side, but without saying any more to each other, they moved across the sunlit car park and into the welcome shade of the building. Inside, they parted.

Rupert, once back in the relative privacy of his surgery, had time to think. He had a clear idea of what had happened that morning, and what had triggered off his uncharacteristic behaviour. He, who had suggested that Antonia should be approached to fill the nursing vacancy, had quite unexpectedly found it difficult to be with her in a working environment. His love for her, which he knew he must keep hidden, had overwhelmed him, and the knowledge that he would be working beside her day by day, while guarding against giving himself away, was suddenly intolerable.

For an hour or two this morning he had wished with all his heart that he had never met Antonia King, with her silver hair and golden tan and solemn grey eyes. He resented falling in love, having resisted it all these years, and then to fall in love with a young and vulnerable woman who needed treating with kid gloves was too much.

And he had, by his own actions, compounded the

problem. He had agreed to stay in Peckhurst for six months to collate evidence about urban medicine, when he might have moved from practice to practice all over the country.

On top of that, he had been idiot enough to suggest to Morris that Antonia should work at the surgery. Yes, it was right for her, a step forward, a road back to normality, but surely he could have left well alone. She'd made a start at the tennis club, and she played like a dream; they played together as if they had been partners for years. Why the hell couldn't he have left it at that, and not brought her here where she was a constant reminder of his own vulnerability? Why indeed?

He had been sufficiently shocked by the feeling of resentment, as they set out for the holiday camp, not to be able to conceal it completely—hence his abrupt manner. Well, now he must come to terms with the situation. His fate was sealed as far as Antonia was concerned; he was irrevocably and totally in love with her. She wasn't aware of this, she didn't know that his heart turned over whenever he looked at her or whenever he heard her voice. Somehow he would, and must, recover his poise and adjust to her daily presence in this close-knit working environment.

He just needed a little time. Above all, he must conceal his feelings for her until she was further along the road to recovery from whatever bitter experience had altered her life.

Well, only a few days ago he had been certain he had endless patience to achieve his goal. He must abide by this, and exercise this virtue and all the self-control he could muster to eventually win her complete trust.

Toni returned to her work in the clinic-room, still rather bemused by Rupert's words and actions that morning. She was pleased they had parted amicably, but still no wiser as to why he had behaved as he had at the camp, or later in the car.

Regarding the car episode, she was also puzzled by her own response to him. Why had his dark, penetrating gaze half frightened, half intrigued her and yet made it possible for her to accept his touch without recoiling? Why, in spite of his unexpected behaviour and her recent distrust of men, did she trust him implicitly?

She couldn't answer any of these questions. Perhaps all would become clear in time. Meanwhile, she told herself, she would enjoy her new life to the full, and try to be prepared for whatever might come her way.

She was sure of one thing—there was to be no turning back now. Perhaps she would falter occasionally on her way to rediscovering herself, but she wouldn't give in. No way was she going to return to the hermit-like way of life she had been living before Rupert appeared and brought her to her senses. She had needed time to adjust to the trauma of rejection by her fiancé, and the death of her grandmother, but it had gone on too long. She must come to terms with life. Duty and courage were her grandfather's watchwords, and perhaps they weren't such bad precepts to follow. Good old-fashioned morals and a bit of backbone, that was what she needed now.

She felt better after she had given herself this little talking-to, and literally squaring her shoulders, geared herself for the rest of the day's work.

She examined her day book of appointments. There were two ECGs to do early in the afternoon. She gave the machine and its attachments a check over to make sure that everything was in order for the first patient, then went out to join Bridget and some of the other staff for a pub lunch at the Drovers.

In the afternoon, after carrying out the ECGs on

the possible cardiac stress patients, she assisted in the pre-school clinic. This was taken by Dr Pat MacNiece, who examined each child prior to their starting school in the autumn. It was all part of an effort to promote healthy family life, and the brainchild of old Dr Meredith.

As well as removing clothes from sometimes reluctant small bodies, it was Toni's duty to weigh each child and check their immunisation cards to make sure all their injections and vaccinations were up to date.

One little girl, Susie Hoskins, a five-year-old, arrived with her mother at the end of the session.

'Can you see her?' Toni asked Pat, who was tidying things away into her case, obviously on the point of leaving. 'I think she's from the encampment on South Lane.'

This was the area that the council had been legally required to provide for travellers. It was a lane that ran through the woods on the outskirts of the town, and there had been much controversy about it being earmarked for travellers, or gypsies as most people still called the caravan dwellers. But it existed, and was properly maintained, and the children were entitled to receive medical and educational care while they were in the district.

'OK, wheel her in,' said Pat rather wearily.

Toni brought the mother and child into the surgery.

Mrs Hoskins was aggressive from the word go. 'I dunno why I 'ave to bring Suse in t'see you,' she complained to the doctor before she had even sat down. 'I've only dun it because the 'eadmistress at the school won't take 'er next term unless she's 'ad a medical check. I think it's a cheek. Why should Suse 'ave to 'ave a check? There's nuthink wrong with 'er.'

'We try to make sure that all children in the district have a medical before they start primary school,' Pat MacNiece explained. 'It means that they start off with a clean bill of health, or if there's anything wrong with their sight or hearing, for instance, it can be dealt with before they begin and they don't miss out at school. It's much better all round.'

'Well, it seems an 'ell of a lot of bother for nuthink to me. I din't 'ave nun of this wiv the others, they just went to school wherever we was, no big deal.' Mrs Hoskins turned to Susie, who seemed not in the least concerned about what was going on. She had her big brown eyes fixed on Toni, apparently fascinated by her coil of hair on which perched her nursing cap. 'Come on, then, Suse, get your fings orf for the doctor.'

Obediently Susie began unbuttoning her blouse, which looked a bit the worse for wear, but clean enough.

'Can I help?' asked Toni, giving the child a nice smile.

Susie nodded, and then as Toni crouched down to her level she put out a small hand and carefully touched the flaxen coronet. 'I like your 'air,' she whispered, 'and the way your 'at goes on the top.'

'Well, thank you very much,' smiled Toni, touched by the child's remark and innocent admiration. 'You've got nice hair too, all black and curly. I used to wish I had black curly hair when I was a little girl.'

'Did you, honest?'

'Honest.' She and Susie exchanged smiles and established an immediate rapport with each other.

While Pat examined Susie, Toni asked Mrs Hoskins, without much hope, if she had brought along Susie's immunisation card.

'I've got it 'ere,' said Mrs Hoskins, and handed over the card, carefully wrapped in a piece of plastic. It was surprisingly clean, and, even more surprising, it was up to date. All the jabs and vaccinations were recorded, and the only unusual thing about the entries was that they extended from Aberdeen to Truro and Deal to Cardiff.

The examination completed, and Susie found to be, as her mother had insisted, fit and well, the pair left, with Susie's voice floating down the corridor.

'Wasn't she nice, Mum, that nurse with the silvery gold 'air? It was like a crown on top of 'er 'ead, like a princess,' she sighed loudly. 'I wish. . .' The shrill little voice faded as mother and daughter passed through the vestibule doors.

'You've certainly made a hit there,' said Pat, grinning as Toni blushed. Her voice assumed an amused edge. 'Felling 'em like ninepins today, King, aren't you, the young and the not so young.'

'What on earth do you mean, MacNiece?' queried Toni, deliberately using the school form of address as her old friend had done.

'Oh, nothing, just a mild observation.' Pat grinned even more broadly. 'I say, isn't that Rupert whizzing off?' She opened the window blinds a little and watched Rupert drive out of the car park. 'How did it go this morning, by the way, the food poisoning at the holiday camp?'

'Fine, everything under control.' So that was it, Toni thought. Pat's letting me know she witnessed the little charade in Rupert's car this morning when we came back from the camp.

'I s-suppose it's no good saying we're just good f-friends?' She silently cursed her stammer. 'Even if it's true?'

Pat swung her surgery case off her desk and put a hand on Toni's shoulder. 'Don't be so damned defensive, old thing. I, and I'm sure all your real friends, would be delighted if you were *not* just good friends. My God, you deserve a break if anyone does, and our Rupert's great material.' She strode towards the door and turned, smiling. "Night, thanks for your help. See you tomorrow—nice to have you aboard.'

Toni tidied Pat's surgery before going through to the clinic-room and checking that all was straight for the morning in a dreamlike state. Her mind seemed to have stayed on hold since Pat had alluded to the car incident.

Who else might have witnessed what was an innocent episode but invested it with a much deeper meaning? And if anyone else had been privy to it, would they be as tolerant, generous even, as Pat MacNiece had been? Several of the other nurses and receptionists had shown signs of being interested in Dr Devenish; would they take kindly to possible competition? Not that she was competing for his favours, of course, but would they believe her? The last thing she wanted, after just having steeled herself to resume work, was any aggro.

It was, however, quite heartwarming to think that her old schoolfriend was rooting for her so strongly and was certainly not herself in the market for Rupert Devenish.

She drove home in a happy frame of mind, finding she was able to quell most of her doubts about the morning episode with Rupert and Pat's subsequent comments. Being back in the world of nursing, although she had as yet only scraped the surface, was exhilarating. She put on Radio Three and was delighted to hear the crashes and bangs of the '1812 Overture' thundering out. It wonderfully complemented her triumphant mood.

There was no tennis match that night, so she spent the evening regaling her grandfather with gossip from the Health Centre. He seemed really interested in what she had to say, and since so many people who were registered with the practice were known to him he was genuinely absorbed by the little titbits of news that Toni passed on to him. For the first time since her grandmother had died, Toni felt she and her grandfather were on the same wavelength, and content in each other's company.

She decided, as she settled for the night, that her first full day's nursing had been a success, overall. Apart from a dodgy hour or so with Rupert at the holiday camp, all had gone well. She even felt equal to facing up to any challenges that might come from other staff keen on Dr Devenish. She would take life one day at a time.

'*Courage, mon ami*,' she said to herself with a giggle and in a strong French accent, just before drifting off to sleep.

The following day passed uneventfully and happily for Toni. Pat MacNiece made no further remarks about the car episode, and Rupert behaved towards Toni almost the same as he did towards everyone else. Just occasionally she caught him looking at her in a rather enigmatic fashion, but each time this happened he turned the look into a smile and said something quite innocuous, so that she was never absolutely sure whether she had imagined anything remarkable.

On Wednesday Toni was on duty from two to seven. She was expected to help out both in reception and in the pharmacy if necessary. She quite enjoyed the change from her clinic-room work, where all routine tests were carried out during the morning or early afternoon. By five o'clock, when the waiting-room began to fill up with patients for the evening surgeries, she was free to help out generally, unless asked by a doctor to attend to a patient.

She knew many of the patients who arrived at the surgery, and it gave her a glow when so many of them said how pleased they were to see her there. Several of them asked after her grandfather, and expressed sympathy for him over his wife's death.

It was just before seven, as Toni was helping Sheila to begin tidying away medical records and forms that had come back from the doctors' rooms after they had seen patients, when there was the sound of a commotion in the vestibule.

'We'd better see what that's all about,' said Sheila, pursing her lips in disapproval and shaking her grey-brown curls.

'I'll go,' said Toni.

The spectacle that met her was quite frightening. Two hefty men, one in his twenties and one middle-aged, were fighting, literally hitting each other with their bare fists. What was even more frightening was that there was a youngish woman, with a small child in a pushchair, who seemed to be trapped between them.

Toni shouted to Sheila over her shoulder, 'Get Rupert and Frank. There's a fight.'

Even with all that was going on, she found a moment to be glad that Rupert and Frank Morgan, the two fittest and reasonably young GPs, were on duty. But her immediate concern was for the red-haired woman and child.

She pulled at the pushchair. 'Come on,' she shouted. 'Come in.'

The woman shook her head. She looked terrified, but refused to budge, tears streaming down her face. 'No—go away!' she shouted back. 'I'll bloody stop them.' She put her hands above her head and tried to catch at the flailing arms of the men. She shrieked at them, but they didn't hear, or didn't take any notice.

Toni tugged at the pushchair, but it was stuck between the legs of the fighting men and she couldn't move it. She stretched forward and bent low over the child, restrained by straps. With fumbling fingers she struggled with the hooks on the webbing. The baby, by now thoroughly frightened, was bawling its head off, and Toni made silly, soothing noises as she tried to release him. One hook seemed to have jammed. At last it came free with a jerk, and she lifted the small boy from the chair.

Rupert and Frank were right behind her as she turned. They didn't ask questions.

She carried the screaming child through the waiting-room, where the few remaining patients were on their feet, looking enquiringly towards the door.

'Shall I give an 'and?' asked one young man, his eyes glowing with anticipation of a scrap. His left leg was in a below-knee plaster.

Toni managed a smile of sorts. 'I think you've got a bit of a handicap,' she said, nodding towards his cast.

'But there's nothin' wrong with these, Nurse,' he said, waving his arms about.

'Just hold off for a bit,' said Toni as she carried the child through to the treatment-room.

A few minutes later Sheila appeared, leading the young woman who had been in the middle of the fight.

'This is Betty,' she said to Toni in a bewildered voice. 'Mrs Taylor, Jason's mother.' She nodded at the bundle that Toni was holding against her shoulder.

'Oh, my baby—give 'im 'ere!' said Mrs Taylor, almost snatching him from Toni's arms.

'Are you all right?' Sheila asked Toni in a loud whisper.

'I'm fine,' Toni reassured her. And then, really quietly, 'Where are the men?'

'One's in with Dr Devenish, the other with Dr Morgan. Look, can I do anything?'

Toni was glad she'd asked. She wasn't yet quite sure how the hierarchy worked at the Centre, and didn't know if she should make suggestions, let alone give orders. But she did know that Mrs Taylor and baby Jason needed something by way of a stimulant.

'What about some tea for Mrs Taylor?' she said.
'And orange juice or milk for the baby?'

'Great—I'll have it ready in a jiff. I bet you could
do with a cup too,' said Sheila.

'I certainly could, but I'd better see if either of the
doctors need me.' Toni realised she was shaking,
presumably with delayed shock.

At that moment, Rupert opened the door of his
room. 'Ah, Nurse.' He smiled at Toni. 'Can you spare
a minute, please?' His voice was professional, but his
smile and the expression in his eyes was not. Then,
quietly so that the man in the room behind him
wouldn't hear, 'Antonia, are you all right, my dear?'

She returned his smile, and clasped her trembling
hands together. 'Of course, Doctor, I'm fine. What
can I do to help?'

'Bring me a couple of sterile dressings and some
narrow strapping, please, and stay and give me a hand
with Mr Lennard.'

'Yes, of course.'

They smiled at each other again, intimate, reassuring smiles in the seclusion of the corridor. Each was
aware that there was something very special about the
moment, perhaps because of their brush with violence,
even though neither of them had been in any real
danger. 'I'll get those things,' murmured Toni, and
turned away down the corridor. She was feeling unac-
countably happy.

When she returned, she cleaned the man's grazed
and cut knuckles with antiseptic and applied a dressing
to one hand, which was quite badly damaged. While
she was doing this, Rupert worked gently on a deep
cut over the man's left eye.

'I'm going to put a few stitches in this cut, Mr
Lennard, after I've given you a local. You won't feel
much more than a prick.'

The man growled, 'Get on with it, then, I ain't got

all day.' He jerked his head from under Rupert's hands and glared and Toni. 'And don't you let that bugger get 'old of my girl or the kid. You keep 'er safe till I'm ready to go, d'ya 'ear?'

Rupert's face went still as a mask and his eyes like chips of dark blue ice. He bent over the man, and for one wild moment Toni thought he was going to strike him.

'Rupert—don't, please.' She laid a hand on his arm. 'You might get. . .' She realised that her concern was for Rupert, not the patient, who was big and burly, and looked ready to kill anyone who got in his way.

Rupert straightened up and looked her full in the face. His own face softened, and his eyes unfroze. He raised his well marked eyebrows. 'Worried about me, Antonia?' he asked softly. And then, in a voice of steel to the patient, 'I understand your concern for your daughter, Mr Lennard, but nobody talks to Nurse King as you did. I want an apology—now!' he rasped out.

The man was clearly taken aback by Rupert's fierceness, and in a grumbling, ungracious manner, muttered that he was sorry. But he was still belligerent. 'But I don't want that bastard getting at her—'e's rubbish, 'e's no bloody good.'

Before Rupert could intervene again, Toni said in a quiet, controlled voice, 'Look, Mr Lennard, your daughter's safe at the moment. She's having a cup of tea with the receptionist. But I can't stop her going off with whoever she wants to if she insists. But she's welcome to stay here until you're ready to leave, if that's what she wants to do.'

''Course it's what she wants ter do. That's why I came with 'er tonight, in case 'e showed up and tried to grab 'er and the kid.'

Rupert, who had remained quiet during this exchange but had applied a local anaesthetic to Mr

Lennard's cheekbone round the cut, asked, 'Is this man a relative—husband, child's father?'

'No, 'e ain't.'

'So, he's forcing himself on your daughter?'

'Yeah, 'e bloody is.'

'Right, this is a case for the police, Mr Lennard. It would have saved a lot of bother and you some damage if you'd called them in before,' said Rupert, and, though his words were severe, his tone had softened. He obviously had sympathy for the man now that he knew more about the situation. 'As soon as I've finished this little job, I'm going to give the local station a ring.'

'My girl won't like that. She feels sorry for the bloke—I ask yer, sorry for 'im. That's why I ain't called in the coppers before. She wouldn't let me.'

'Well,' said Rupert grimly, 'your daughter doesn't have any say in the matter at the moment. I'm phoning about a disturbance on Health Centre property, and a threat to my patients.'

Much later, the Health Centre was quiet and empty, apart from the staff kitchen, where Toni and Sheila and the two doctors sat drinking hot sweet tea and demolishing ginger biscuits.

The late evening sun was streaming through the windows with long red-gold fingers of warmth and light. All four of them were slowly recovering from the traumatic effects of the fight that had taken place on their doorstep.

The police had come, taken statements and gone away, taking Hicks, the man who had tried to grab the girl and her baby, with them. They might, they said, be back again tomorrow for more information.

'Funny thing,' said Frank, 'the way love takes people and the way it's so often mixed up with violence.'

Sheila said in a wavery little voice, still clearly upset

by what had happened, 'I don't understand how people can be like that. Don and I hardly had a cross word all our married life. Yet he's gone, and people like that. . .' She shook her head and tears welled up in her pale blue eyes. 'I'm sorry,' she said, 'making a fool of myself.' She managed a smile. 'I'd better get off home before I really go to pieces. But I would just like to say how marvellous I think you all were, dealing with them.'

'Sheila, your tea was a lifesaver, and you were super with that poor girl and the child. You're allowed to go to pieces now, we're all friends and colleagues, for heaven's sake.' Rupert put a large arm round the receptionist and squeezed her shoulder. 'I think it's time we all went home,' he said.

Frank sprang up from the table. 'Bloody hell, I'm on call tonight, and an early start tomorrow. Sheila, I'll give you a lift, it's on my way. Perhaps you can spare a poor hard-working doctor a cup of coffee and something more substantial than this.' He indicated the empty biscuit pack.

Toni and Rupert, and probably Sheila too, knew that Frank Morgan was making sure she was not alone in the house for a while when she reached home.

A few minutes later they were all in the car park, waving each other off.

'See you tomorrow, Antonia,' said Rupert softly as Toni climbed into the Land Rover. 'You sure you're all right?' he looked concerned.

'Fine,' she smiled. 'I'm just fine,' she said, and waved as she drove off.

CHAPTER NINE

FOLLOWING the punch-up at the Health Centre, life seemed to settle down into a regular pattern for Toni, almost equally divided between nursing and tennis practice. It was just as well that the high summer season meant less work in the hothouses, because she had less time to spend there.

It was the shop, mail order business and the big tunnel greenhouses that were busy at this time of year.

Working very early in the light summer mornings, or sometimes late in the golden evenings, to keep things ticking over, suited her very well. The solitude and quiet of the hothouses contrasted wonderfully with the busy, often noisy Health Centre. In a way, she realised, it very much complemented her own feelings and emerging emotions. She enjoyed the stimulus of working with other people, accepting and dealing with problems, but there were times when she wanted to retreat into a corner and mull things over.

One of the most satisfying ingredients of her new life was, without doubt, Rupert Devenish. The fight episode had added a new dimension to their relationship. Each knew that the other cared. For Toni, the knowledge that he was close to her without posing a sexual threat had been enhanced by the events of that night. He had been both strong and gentle, with her and with Sheila, and for that matter with Mrs Taylor, her father and her baby. She had seen, as it were, the whole man in action, protecting, advising and comforting.

* * *

For Rupert, the fight and its aftermath had provided a glimpse of an Antonia who was fast coming to terms with herself, and who cared, at least a little, if perhaps unconsciously, about him. The realisation filled him with elation. He could wait for as long as it took for her to want him as badly as he wanted her, and deep down in his bones he was sure it would happen. He and Antonia made a splendid partnership both at work and on the tennis court, and one day, please God, that would be translated into a partnership for life.

As Frank Morgan had said that night, love was a strange emotion and had an even stranger way of refining and declaring itself.

The waiting-room, or rather its occupants, especially in the evenings, subtly changed as high summer progressed. There was still, in this community containing a preponderance of retired folk and a fair number of children from the sprawling council estate, the usual coughs, colds and painful joints, but now a different sort of patient began to show up—holidaymakers, locals preparing to go off to exotic locations and requiring anti-everything jabs, and incoming visitors arriving from all over the place, bringing with them an array of minor injuries, from sprained wrists to sunburn.

'Well, look what's blown into town,' said Bridget one evening in a pseudo-Western drawl, as two mahogany-brown men entered the vestibule. This year virtually everyone had a tan owing to the heatwave that had started in April, but nobody locally could compete with this deep leathery brown acquired after months at sea. 'Sailors ahoy. Some of the more serious of the yachting fraternity,' went on the irrepressible Bridget, 'back from the Aegean or the Indian Ocean filled to the gunwales with duty-free or other contraband.'

It wasn't only their tans that gave them away; they

wore espadrilles, very short shorts, showing off muscular thighs, and spoke with the brittle, loud, over-confident accents that went with luxury yachts and unlimited time to enjoy them.

Toni, who was on duty to give a hand wherever needed, nipped round from the pharmacy department to reception.

'Good evening, can I help?' she asked one of the Greek gods who appeared at the desk.

'Well, honey, you just about can, any way you please.'

The phoney Deep South accent was revolting, thought Toni, not funny as Bridget's had been. It was accompanied by an insolent, appraising look that she found offensive. She stared at the man with her cool grey eyes.

'You need to see a doctor?'

He persisted with the assumed accent, but, taken rather aback by her coolness, modified his approach.

'I sure do, ma'am, or rather, my friend here does. They told us down at the clubhouse that the medicos here would take us aboard.'

'Yes, you can sign on as temporary residents, but if you want to see a doctor tonight I'm afraid you'll have to wait till surgery's finished, unless there's a cancellation.'

'You mean we have to wait here?' asked the Greek god, shocked out of his accent.

'Frightfully sorry, 'fraid so,' replied Toni in her best county voice, giving the man a ravishing smile. 'Now, if you'd complete these forms, please,' she pushed the temporary resident forms across the counter, 'I'll let you know as soon as a doctor is free.'

'Look here,' began the man, leaning against the glass panel, and fractionally lowering his voice, 'we can pay, y'know.'

'Oh, good,' said Toni. 'But I'm afraid you'll still have to wait. We don't allow queue-jumping.'

The man grabbed the forms and returned to his companion, who was leaning against a window-ledge, ignoring the last empty chair. They had a whispered conference, then both came back to the desk. Toni saw that the second man was limping, and close up could see that he was pale and sweating beneath his tan.

She said sharply to the first man, 'Your friend looks ill—you should have told me.' Through her mind flashed all sorts of awful possibilities, most of them variations on the variety of diseases that the traveller might have picked up in the tropics. 'You'd better come through here.' She led the way to the clinic-room. 'Now, Mr. . .?'

'Woodward, James.'

'Mr Woodward, you don't look very well.' No longer interested in the other man and his silly play-acting, Toni was her usual professional self. She gave Mr Woodward a reassuring smile. 'I'll get a doctor to see you as soon as possible. Meanwhile, if you'd like to sit here. . .' She indicated the chair by her desk. 'Make yourself comfortable.'

James Woodward looked acutely embarrassed, and his companion suppressed a laugh. 'Sorry, Nurse, I can't sit down—well, not properly. I've got a boil or something on my b. . . on my behind and it's giving me hell!'

Toni's first reaction was one of relief that the man didn't have some scary tropical disease, but this gave way to concern. A boil on the bottom might sound music-hall funny, but, untreated and infected, could be serious. And Mr Woodward certainly looked as if he was running a temperature, typical with an infection.

'I'll fetch a doctor,' she said firmly. 'You go behind

the screen, take off your shorts and lie face downwards on the couch, and you, Mr. . . ?'

'Francis Formby.'

'Can go back to the waiting-room.'

'Oh, I say,' he grinned broadly, flashing healthy-looking white teeth at her. 'Can't I stay and see the fun? You don't mind, James, do you?'

'There's nothing funny about having an infected boil,' Toni said severely, pushing the man towards the door. In the corridor she hissed at him, 'This could be serious for your friend, you know, not a laughing matter.'

'You're kidding! A boil, serious?'

'Not kidding, Mr Formby. Now, please, the waiting-room.'

A patient was just leaving Rupert's room, and Toni nipped in before he could buzz for anyone else.

He gave her a slow, welcoming smile that lit up the intense blue of his eyes which crinkled at the corners. 'Antonia, how nice. What brings you hither, work or pleasure?' he teased.

The warmth of his greeting pleased her immensely.

'Work, I'm afraid.' And for a moment she wished it weren't. Rupert seemed so very pleased to see her, as if they hadn't met for days, instead of just an hour or so ago. She explained about James Woodward and his boil.

'Oh, poor chap. I'll be along in a couple of minutes. Could you take his temp and pulse for me, and set up a tray with whatever you think I may need to treat it? Scalpel, sterile-dressing pack, ribbon gauze for drainage and so on. And something in the antibiotic line. You might find out if he's allergic to the penicillin group, they're very useful in this field.'

Mr Woodward was lying as Toni had instructed on his stomach. He was wearing the briefest of pants and on the right side these were badly stained with blood and pus. Radiating from the edge of his briefs was a red, angry-looking area of skin, trailing down the back of his thigh.

'I'm going to take your temperature and pulse while we're waiting for the doctor,' Toni explained, 'and then I'll soak off your pants where they're stuck to the skin, but I may have to cut them away. They're pretty well ruined anyway, I'm afraid.' Not, she was sure, that the loss of a pair of pants would bother him.

'It doesn't matter. Will the doc be long?' Whatever bravado he'd put on earlier had evaporated, and he looked exhausted.

'No, and he'll give you something for the pain as soon as he's examined you. Here, let me pop the thermometer in your mouth.' He parted cracked lips.

While the thermometer was cooking, Toni took his pulse. It was fast, though quite strong. She scribbled 120 on a pad, and later recorded his temperature beside it as 38.5C—high enough.

'Are you allergic to penicillin?' she asked. He shook his head. She began to lay up a trolley. 'And when did this boil start?'

'Oh, a month or so ago. We were off the coast of Sardinia and we did a long haul ashore in the dinghy. I was hot and sweaty and I guess the seat was gritty. It itched a bit for a day or so, then produced a lump. I put some antiseptic cream on it that we had in the first-aid cupboard, but it just wouldn't heal, although it's only in the last few days that it's really bothered me, made me quite sick at times. I think it's spread a bit.'

'I think it probably has,' said Toni, making a face which the patient couldn't see, as she soaked off the cotton material with Savlon solution, exposing a large inflamed area with several suppurating points. The boil had escalated into a carbuncle.

In spite of it being a warm evening, Mr Woodward began to shiver. Toni covered him with a cotton cellular blanket, allowing air to circulate over his hot skin without inhibiting his sweating.

Rupert arrived and introduced himself. He took one look at the carbuncle and raised his eyebrows at Toni over the prone figure.

'I think we're going to be just in time to treat this, Mr Woodward. Another hour or two and we'd have had a full-blown case of blood poisoning on our hands.'

The patient groaned and tried to sound laconic. 'Not surprised—it started to give me hell this morning as we came up-Channel. I was sick as a dog—couldn't keep anything down.' He tried a brave grin. 'Can you get me OK for tonight, Doc? There's a super party lined up.'

''Fraid not,' replied Rupert equally laconic. 'No party, no alcohol—rest, tepid baths, gallons of fluid and an injection several times a day for a few days.' He turned to Toni. 'Penicillin OK?' She nodded, and he indicated what he wanted from the trolley.

She drew up into a syringe Penicillin G sodium and opened a vial of pethidine.

'Nurse is going to give you an intramuscular injection of a penicillin-based drug together with a pain-killer, Mr Woodward, that'll begin treating the infection and hopefully reduce the pain and temperature. Then we'll start dealing with this carbuncle.'

Toni gave the injection into the upper and outer quadrant of the left buttock, and massaged the area to help the fluid disperse. Rupert cleaned the affected area on the other buttock and decided on a magnesium sulphate dressing to draw out the septic matter. 'Avoid cutting,' he murmured.

Toni prepared the magnesium and a covering pad which she secured with Micropore tape. James Woodward was already looking fractionally better, just resting. She sponged his face, hands and wrists with cold water. He was obviously immensely fit, a true outdoor sailor type, with blond beard and thick blond wavy hair combed back from his deeply tanned face.

He gave Toni a shaky smile and she found herself smiling back. He's much nicer than his friend, she thought, not nearly so brash. 'Thanks, Nurse,' he said. 'Sorry to have mucked up your evening schedule and your surgery, Doctor.' He turned, as well as he was able in his face-downwards position, to look at Rupert, who was busily writing at the desk.

Rupert's eyes gleamed, then he looked thoughtfully at Toni before he spoke.

'Think nothing of it,' he said in a flat impersonal tone. 'That's what we're here for. But we've now got to sort out your treatment over the next few days. You need professional care while you're having these large injections to fight off the infection, and until your temperature comes down. A boat, however luxurious, isn't really the place for you, especially as your companion probably wants to live it up for a bit, now you're in the marina. I don't think it would be fair to either of you for you to stay aboard—cramp his style and delay your recovery.'

'I'll do whatever you suggest, Doctor. You're right, of course, about plans to live it up. Thanks for being so understanding.'

Rupert shrugged. 'I've done a bit of sailing in my time, in the distant days of my youth.' He sounded dispirited, Toni thought, and bitter, though she couldn't think why. She wished he wouldn't harp on his age, whatever that was; he looked as lean and fit as James Woodward might at his best.

'You look as if you could still do a bit of useful crewing,' said the younger man, confirming her thoughts. 'Now what do you want me to do?'

It was decided that he should be admitted to the private nursing home nearby, provided they had a room available. They had, and a few minutes later a rather chastened Mr Formby helped his friend into his hired car and drove him to the nursing home.

Toni had seen them off, and James Woodward, half sitting, half lying on the back seat, had thanked her again for the care she had given him. 'Please come and visit me in the nursing home,' he begged. 'Francis will be too busy and probably too drunk after tonight's party to come and see me, and I shall be all on my own.'

'For heaven's sake, you're only in for a few days, and Matron may not let you have visitors. She's an old dragon,' Toni lied cheerfully. 'She'll probably insist on complete bed-rest and keep you incommunicado while you're her patient.'

'I say, she won't, will she?' Francis Formby asked in a horrified voice. 'I'm glad it's you and not me who's entering those portals.'

James ignored him. 'You will come, won't you?' he pleaded.

'I'll consider it. I might,' answered Toni as she stepped back from the car and smiled and waved a goodbye.

Rupert came to the door of the clinic-room as she was tidying up. 'Nice young chap, that James Woodward. I hope he responds to treatment.'

Toni felt faintly alarmed. 'Why, is there any reason why he shouldn't?' she queried.

'No,' replied Rupert thoughtfully. 'Not really. I just have a feeling, quite unjustified, I'm sure. I think I'll pop into Rowans on my way up to the club.' He looked at Toni with unseeing eyes. 'Perhaps,' he mulled over, partly to himself, partly to her, 'he's more dehydrated than I thought—vomiting and heat. Perhaps a drip. Yes, that might help.' He smiled, clearly relieved to have found something constructive to do. 'See you on court at about half-past eight, Antonia, that suit you?'

He turned abruptly and left the room, anxious to

get back to his patients and then to the nursing home
to prepare a drip for James Woodward.

'Yes, of course,' she answered to his retreating back,
for some reason feeling shut out of his thoughts, and
for once, of little consequence to him. She shivered.
She didn't like the sensation at all.

Resolutely she shook it off. That was simply the
good doctor in him, putting patients before personal
considerations. She was not, in any case, quite sure
whether Rupert had been distant or not, or whether
she had simply imagined it. He remained as enigmatic
now as he had when she first met him, and she knew
very little more about him personally than she had
then.

He wasn't married. His home, not the cottage that
he rented on the edge of Peckhurst, was near Dorking.
Somewhere along the grapevine she had heard that it
was large and grand, and his widowed mother and his
sister-in-law and her children lived there too.

'His ancestral home, almost like a castle,' someone
had said. 'His elder brother is a baronet, I believe.
He's an explorer or something, away a lot.'

The conversation had made Toni feel uncomfortable, as if she was spying on the man, and she had
changed the subject quickly. Not that she had insti-
gated it, the information had simply emerged.

She could have found out more about Rupert
Devenish from Uncle Morris, or even Grandfather,
but the same feeling of intruding on his private life
prevented her. It was sufficient to know that both
these elderly gentlemen thought highly of him, but it
would, she occasionally thought rather wistfully, have
been nice if he had wanted to tell her more about
himself.

Not that there was much opportunity for intimate
conversation. Except at the tennis club she didn't meet
him much socially. She fraternised mostly with her old

schoolfriends and their partners, and his limited free
time was spent at his London flat, the teaching hospital, and his Dorking home.

She presumed he had friends in London, probably
dry-as-dust professors of medicine and superior con-
sultants. They'd probably bore me to death, she
decided, if I ever got around to meeting them. An
unpalatable thought struck her—perhaps Rupert
found her and her friends boring. Maybe they were
too young and silly for him, not intellectual enough.
Because he enjoyed playing tennis, and they were
keen players, he tolerated them at the club, where
there were also older members for him to chat with if
he wished.

Toni went to bed on the thought that night. It was
Rupert's fault, this obsession with the difference in
their ages, and she wished he wouldn't keep making
references to it. This afternoon in the clinic-room he'd
pretended to be too ancient for sailing. What a load of
rubbish. Even James Woodward had seen through
that.

James Woodward! Perhaps she would visit him at
the nursing home. He really was rather nice, and very
handsome, even if ill and sweating with fever, and with
a carbuncle on his buttock. She was so glad he was
improving.

'He didn't need a drip after all,' Rupert had told her
when he joined her at the club. 'Matron said he was
taking in gallons of squash, and responding accordingly. Of course, he's young and fit.' Another refer-
ence to age, Toni had thought crossly. 'By the way, he
wants you to visit him. I said I'd pass on the message.'

He hit a few balls hard across the net as they
knocked up, then played Toni and the opposing pair
almost to a standstill by the end of the evening.

He seemed cross and rather fed-up, she thought,

not a bit like his usual self. She wished that there was something she could do to cheer him up, but fell asleep before deciding how or what.

She realised the following day that it didn't matter that she hadn't come up with a solution. Rupert was back to normal, calm, full of good humour and as always wonderful with his patients.

'Our divine Dr Devenish is in great form today, isn't he?' said one of the community nurses to Toni. 'Smashing guy. I wish I was ten years younger, I'd go for him in a big way. Of course, it would also help if I didn't have three teenage kids and a demanding husband.' She grinned happily and went off on her rounds.

Age! thought Toni irritably; everyone seems to be obsessed by age. She banged a few receivers about and felt better, then went through to the waiting-room to collect her first patient of the day.

CHAPTER TEN

TONI toyed with the idea of visiting James Woodward over the next few days. He had seemed keen to see her again, and must be finding it rotten being ill when he should have been enjoying the hectic social life that the marina offered. She didn't think his friend Francis would take visiting too seriously. He definitely wasn't the type to miss out on his pleasures while in port. And James was attractive. It would be an opportunity to prove to herself that she was on the mend, if she did something positive towards getting to know him better.

It was Rupert who, in the end, decided the matter for her. She hadn't seen anything of him for a couple of days as he'd been lecturing in London, and she experienced a little jolt of pleasure at the sight of him. He was seeing a patient from his room, a little old lady, over whom he was bending solicitously as he steered her into the corridor.

'Don't hesitate to come back, Mrs Doyle,' he was saying as Toni approached, 'if the cream doesn't work.'

The little old lady, all of four feet nothing, said something in a fluting voice, to which Rupert replied, 'Only too pleased—any time.'

Toni halted beside him, and together they watched Mrs Doyle toddle away to reception.

Rupert smiled at her. 'Hi,' he said softly, the pleasure at seeing her obvious in his voice. 'I'm glad I bumped into you. I wanted a word, if you've got a moment.'

'Only a moment, I'm afraid.' She smiled back at him

and wished she had more time. She edged a little down the corridor. 'I'm just going to fetch a patient from the waiting-room.'

'Yes, of course, you're busy—we're both busy. Perhaps later.' He half turned back into his office.

How extraordinary, she thought—Rupert hesitating, unsure of himself. She took a step back towards him and touched his arm. 'I don't suppose my patient will mind waiting another minute or two. What did you want to speak to me about?'

He had recovered his usual poise and answered briskly, 'James Woodward. Poor chap, he's still making progress, but it's a slow business. He's had a touch of malaria to add to his problems. Picked it up years ago on a trip to Malawi, and is subject to bouts when at a physical low. He's going to be restricted for longer than we originally thought. You'd be doing him a favour if you visited; his so-called friend and fellow mariner has only been in to see him once. The poor guy's lonely.'

The corridor was long and seemed narrower than it really was, because it stretched the length of the single-story building on one side. There was no one else around. Toni had the odd feeling that they were isolated in time and space in the dimmish light.

It was a sort of no-man's-land, between the patients and the professionals. A green, grey area. Dim in the daytime because light only came through the fanlights above the room doors, dim at night, because the fluorescent tubes functioned on low key, sufficient for movement, but not for close scrutiny.

'Oh, I'm so sorry, what a beastly thing to happen to him,' said Toni. 'As if his carbuncle wasn't enough to contend with! He must be feeling wretched, poor man.' She felt dreadfully guilty. Why hadn't she gone to see James before, or at least rung up to find out how he was?

Rupert leaned closer towards her. His gentian-blue eyes peered down into hers. 'I told you the other evening that he wanted you to visit.' He sounded almost accusing.

'So you did,' she said, anger at the implication that she was at fault overriding her own sense of guilt. 'But I didn't think it was an order—you know, d-doctor's orders. You didn't say.' He seemed intent on showering her with blame. It was ridiculous. Surely he was being almost too concerned about James Woodward, especially as it didn't relate exclusively to his physical well-being.

Her grey eyes challenged his and she willed herself not to look away.

'You know I wasn't suggesting that you had to see him,' he said explosively, and glanced up and down the corridor to make sure they were still alone. 'I wouldn't dream of dictating to you, and what you do when you're off duty is your own affair.' He shrugged and seemed to be groping for words, so unusual for him. 'It's just that it seemed a good idea. He needs company, and you must sometimes get bored stiff with always being with the same crowd. It seemed an opportunity for you both to. . .'

His voice trailed away and he looked down at her in a puzzled fashion, his eyebrows brought together in a ferocious frown. He bent his head down even closer, and for one heart-stopping moment Toni thought he was going to kiss her.

'Oh,' she said softly, soothingly, her anger evaporating at once. To her astonishment, she found herself wishing she had the nerve to reach up and smooth his bunched-up forehead. A wave of such tenderness swept over her that she gasped with surprise. Rupert, usually so strong, so sure, was muddled, unsure. Her voice dropped to a whisper. 'I'm glad you're not insisting that I visit James Woodward. You seemed almost to be throwing me at him.'

He said irritably, 'What nonsense. You must know that such a thought hadn't crossed my mind, but he's young and needs young company. I feel sorry for the chap.' He unknitted his eyebrows, smiled, ran a hand through his thick chestnut hair and squared his wide shoulders. Immediately he seemed his usual confident self. He patted her arm in an avuncular fashion. 'Forget it, it was a stupid idea. Rule number one, don't get too involved with one's patients, it makes for all sorts of problems. I don't know what made me suggest you visit—silly idea.'

Toni smiled up at him. 'I think it's a good idea,' she said brightly, conscious that her cheeks were pink and hoping he wouldn't notice. 'And it's much better to break a few rules because you care. I'll pop in tonight to see him, before going to the club.'

He said, sounding cool and casual, 'Well, if you're sure you don't mind?'

'Positive.' She almost told him that all she minded was his seeming desire to push her into another man's arms. But of course she didn't. She gave him a dazzling smile, said, 'See you,' very cheerfully, and took herself off to the waiting-room.

Rupert watched her swing with her long-legged stride down the corridor, her tailored uniform dress, held round her slim waist by a stiff wide navy blue belt, moulding smoothly over her trim buttocks and twitching rhythmically against the backs of her knees. It reminded him of the day that he had met her and she had preceded him up the steps from the seedhouse to the potting-shed. He had thought then that she had the neatest bottom he'd ever seen, and he thought so still.

With a throaty growl, he turned back into his office, where he sat for several minutes at his desk staring unseeingly at the opposite wall. The receptionist rang through on the internal phone asking diffidently if he was ready for his next patient.

'Yes, of course, send in. . .' he looked at the buff envelope in front of him '. . .Mrs Green.' He took out the sheaf of notes and began reading about the patient's rheumatism and circulatory problems. There was a tap at the door, and he got up and opened it. 'Good morning, Mrs Green, do come in. I'm sorry to have kept you waiting.' He flashed her a smile of apology.

'Oh, that's all right, Doctor, I know how busy you are. You must have such a lot on your mind.'

You can say that again, thought Rupert as he questioned and examined her, and then other patients as the morning progressed. Almost for the first time in his life he found it difficult to suppress his personal problems and concentrate on the job. Somehow he did it. Everyone went away feeling they'd had his full attention and best advice. As one patient said as she was queueing for her medicine at the pharmacy window, 'That Dr Devenish always seems really interested in you. Not impatient like some of them are.'

'Yep, he's good news,' agreed Bridget, handing the packet of tablets through to the elderly lady. 'We're lucky to have him.'

Recalling the conversation he had had with Antonia, and her pertinent remark that he was throwing her together with James Woodward, Rupert acknowledged privately that that was precisely what he was doing. He was deliberately trying to foster a friendship between them. It was a test of some kind. A test for whom, him or Antonia? Even thinking about it made him feel foolish and insecure. What a state he'd allowed himself to get into, mooning like a schoolboy over a woman years younger. How right Morris Meredith had been when he said that a late love was the most difficult and demanding and obsessive of all loves.

Toni too was abstracted for the rest of the day as she took blood, tested urine, gave injections and removed stitches. Because of years of training, she was able to dissemble and appear to her patients to be giving them her undivided attention. But fragments of her meeting and the conversation she'd had with Rupert trickled in and out of her thoughts as she worked.

His uncertainty was intriguing. She hadn't a clue what had caused it. It was strange to see him as anything but sure of himself. True, he had quickly regained his usual phlegm, but it triggered off a line of thought that she hadn't considered before. He had always appeared, in the short time that she had known him, rocklike, indestructible, shrewd, wise—omniscient almost. And yet he had wavered this morning, briefly, and she, inadequate as she felt herself to be, had wanted to comfort him. When they had eyed each other in the dim remoteness of the corridor, and he had bent towards her, she had thought, had hoped, he was going to kiss her.

That in itself was incredible. That she could *want* him to kiss her. Not knowing her history, Rupert wouldn't know why wanting him to kiss her was so remarkable. It was a secret that she must hug to herself, or perhaps discuss with her counsellor, the one person who would appreciate the importance of what had happened.

But why discuss this with anyone? This warm craving to feel Rupert's lips on hers had nothing to do with anyone else, and certainly nothing to do with the gross insult to which she had been subjected by a man in the past. Rupert was a different kind of animal, a caring,

tender person, both as a man and a doctor. There was
no need to analyse her reasons for wanting him to kiss
her; it was the most natural thing in the world for two
people attracted to each other to kiss.

Her visit to James Woodward that evening was brief.
He had had a bad afternoon, with a high temperature
and profuse sweating. When she arrived he was half
dozing.

'The rigor took it out of him,' said the nurse who
fetched Toni from the reception hall. 'But when he
heard you were here, he insisted on seeing you. But
you shouldn't stay too long.'

'I won't,' Toni promised.

James was pathetically pleased to see her. She was
shocked to see him looking quite ill, more so than he
had at the Health Centre that first evening. It was of
course due to the onset of the malaria, which, though
diagnosed as a mild attack, had obviously taken its
toll. Even his dark brown tan couldn't hide the peculiar
sheen that the pyrexia of illness produced on the skin.
No wonder Rupert had been keen for her to visit—his
concern was justified.

With her new-found confidence, Toni bent over the
bed and kissed James on his damp forehead.

'I say,' he said, in a thread of a voice, 'that was
nice.'

She said in a joking fashion, 'Make the most of it. I
don't usually go around kissing comparative strangers.'

He managed a laugh of sorts. 'Anyone who's seen
as much of me as you have can't really be designated a
stranger.'

'I hadn't thought of that. By the way, how's your
poor old BTM?' she asked.

He was lying propped on his left side with a cradle
over his hips.

'I'm told it's coming along nicely, though to be honest it doesn't feel like it, it still hurts like hell.'

'I expect that's because you're below par on account of the malaria.'

'Yeah, it's a damned nuisance. It looks as if I might not be fit enough to move when Francis is ready to weigh anchor. According to your Dr Devenish, I'm going to be pretty useless for the next few weeks.'

'Oh, I am sorry. It must be awful to have your plans mucked up like that.'

'Well,' he said gamely, 'there are compensations, such as being visited by the most beautiful nurse in the UK. It could have happened on some godforsaken island inhabited by scorpions, white ants, and precious little else.'

'Yes, I can see that Peckhurst might be a better bet than that.' Toni brushed her lips against his forehead again. 'Now I'm going to be off. You must rest, but I'll visit again soon.'

He looked at her wistfully. 'Promise?'

'Promise.'

Rupert was at the tennis club before her.

'Did you go and see young Woodward?' he asked directly she appeared.

'Yes. He is poorly, isn't he? I was quite shocked by his appearance.'

'Yes, there's nothing like a good old-fashioned fever to stage a dramatic effect.'

Toni had wondered if it might be difficult, even embarrassing, to meet him that evening after their earlier encounter, but he was his usual self, and after the first few uneasy moments so was she.

They went out on court to do a knock-up while they were waiting for the opposing pair to show up. When they did, Rupert and Toni beat them quickly and easily.

'I feel like playing on,' said Rupert as the other pair prepared to leave the court. 'What about a match between us, or at least as much of a game as the light will allow?'

'I'm on.'

They played through the blue and gold evening, and continued when the blue turned to purple and the gold disc of the sun settled in dusky bands of orange and pink.

The last game was particularly exhilarating, with a lot of net play of the kind that would be useful to them in the doubles. They finished one set all.

'A fitting finale to the day, I think,' said Rupert, joining Toni at the bench.

She was struggling to put on her cardigan, which had got tangled in her ponytail. 'Here, let me help.' With deft fingers he released her hair and smoothed her jacket over her shoulders. And then very casually he turned her to face him.

'Thanks,' she said, smiling up at him.

He returned her smile and inclined his head towards her.

For the second time that day she wondered if he was going to kiss her, and for the second time, Rupert wondered if he dared. He allowed his lips to brush her hair. She trembled. He squeezed her shoulders gently. His eyes gleamed as violet as the dusk around them. He let his lips trail feather-light across her forehead, then stepped back.

That, he felt, was as far as he dared go. A tiny bat flitted around their heads. The dusk deepened, the last bird twittered sleepily. A couple of hundred yards away the lights of the clubhouse glowed cheerfully.

Rupert tied the sleeves of his sweater loosely round his neck and picked up his racket and net of balls. He took her hand in his and raised it to his lips.

'Thank *you*, Antonia, for a wonderful evening,' he

murmured huskily, then cleared his throat. 'One set all—just proves what a good match we are, my dear, doesn't it?' He pressed her hand before releasing it.

'Yes,' she said softly, 'I think perhaps we're an ideal match,' adding hastily, 'Well, on court anyway.'

'Ah, only on court? Perhaps we should work on that?' His voice was deep and resonant.

'Perhaps.' Excitement welled up within her. She tried to damp it down. Too much had happened too soon. She couldn't handle it yet. She needed more time. 'Perhaps,' she repeated, and made her voice sound cool, though friendly. And to show that all was well between them, she slipped her hand into his as they walked along the dark paths back to the clubhouse.

Hot, mainly dry June gave way to the much more mixed month of July. Wimbledon came and went. While it was on, the tennis club members spent their time, between matches for their own little Wimbledon, glued to television sets scattered about the club. Everyone had a favourite and wanted to be a Becker or a Graf, a Martina Navratilova or a Stefan Edberg.

No one, of course, came anywhere near those dizzy heights, but some of the club players were good, and it became increasingly obvious as the season progressed that four of the best players were the mixed doubles pairs who consistently routed their opponents.

It had been an inspiration of Terry Banks' to put them in opposite halves of the draw. Everyone looked foward to the doubles final, which unless anything went disastrously wrong before the middle of August should prove a battle between Kieron Duffry, his partner, Melanie Bean, and Rupert Devenish and Antonia King.

All four were putting in as much practice as possible, turning up early in the morning or late evening to use

the rarely available empty courts. For Toni, the world
had been turned upside down. Suddenly she was back
in the thick of everything, just as she had been in times
past. Her days were filled—three full days and two
half days at the surgery, around which she fitted in
necessary work at the nursery, tennis practice and the
rediscovery of partying and socialising with her
contemporaries.

In anticipation of continuing with her nursing in
some capacity after Mary Mates returned from maternity leave, she began training in one of the girls from
the shop who was interested in the hothouse side of
the work in the nursery.

Felicity Cook, an eighteen-year-old girl who had
worked at King's Seeds since she had left school, was
keen and willing. Toni felt she had a 'natural' to teach.
She felt rather like her grandmother must have felt
when she was teaching her how to handle tiny plants,
and explaining how important it was to keep everything clean and tidy, from the tools to the benches and
trays. It occurred to her that this was not too different
from the attention to orderliness that was a rule in
nursing, a basic necessity.

But much as she enjoyed teaching Felicity, and her
love for growing things, more and more she realised
that her true love was nursing. The days at the Health
Centre were the high points of her week. If Felicity
was a natural in the hothouse, she, Toni, was a natural
in nursing. It wasn't a new discovery, simply a confir-
mation of her years of training.

The Health Centre was a stepping-stone to a return
to hospital nursing at some future date. Such was her
confidence that she could even contemplate the possibility of encountering the despicable Patrick, her ex-
fiancé, on the hospital circuit.

She never forgot that it was Rupert Devenish who
was responsible for persuading her to take those first

few frightened steps back into the world. She would be eternally grateful to him for that, and for turning out to be a man of honour, which for a while she had doubted. But in spite of feeling so close to him, and at times expecting more from their relationship, especially after the magic end to the day when they had played tennis into the dusky twilight, she no longer needed his constant reassurance.

The whispery, romantic feeling she'd had for him when James Woodward was resident in the nursing home had faded, perhaps disappeared completely.

Nothing had come out of the moment when she thought he wanted to kiss her, and she wanted to receive his kiss. He wasn't exactly aloof after that episode, but he was guarded on the rare occasions that they were alone together, as if he too had had second thoughts about developing their friendship.

Daily contact was enough. To know that he was around was sufficient, to partner him at tennis was a delight. They were a perfect match, just as they were well matched in the surgery, combining cool professionalism with a warm and caring quality.

His spiky and strange behaviour of the first morning when they had worked together weeks before had seldom been repeated. Generally, he now treated Toni as he did all the other staff, with courtesy and cheerful friendliness, though at times rather more distantly than she would have wished. It was as if he sometimes wanted to say something, and didn't, or couldn't, and, to hide the fact, retreated a little, but only ever briefly, soon returning to normal.

Rupert had, over the last few weeks, started a special clinic. Or rather it had come about almost by accident. The other doctors at the Centre, realising that he was an expert in the field of tissue damage, began asking him to see patients with ulcers. These were mostly on legs, varicose ulcers, with a few on heels and elbows, and, when the community nurses reported cases of bed-bound patients, sacral sores.

There were many improved healing packs on the market, most of which were highly efficient if properly prescribed and used. The skill came in assessing which dressing would suit each ulcer, and following through the treatment to the bitter end, sometimes changing one form of dressing for another at a certain point.

As clinic nurse, Toni found herself much involved with this work. Because of the growing numbers of patients being diverted to Rupert, it made sense to set aside one afternoon a week to examine, diagnose and treat these patients. So every Wednesday, the clinic-room was given over to this special session.

It was rather like being back in hospital, Toni thought, as she settled Mrs Jackson, who was the last patient of the day, behind the screen that temporarily divided the room. This method allowed Rupert to examine patients one side and her to do treatments the other. It was a time-saver. He could tell her exactly what he wanted done as soon as he had seen a patient, and she had the facilities to carry out his instructions immediately and fill in the record card and arrange follow-up visits.

On this particular Wednesday, the last in July, Rupert came round the screen, flicked Toni a quick smile and turned to the patient.

'Nurse is going to put a special antiseptic jelly on this ankle ulcer, Mrs Jackson. It's bright green, looks a bit lurid, but it does a wonderful job of deep-cleaning wounds like yours. It's also convenient, because once a sterile dressing has been secured over the top it won't have to be touched for a week. I'll leave Nurse to sort out your next visit, when I hope there'll be a great improvement.' He bent over the couch and shook the lady's hand. 'Goodbye, Mrs Jackson, see you next week.'

Toni thought, he's so kind and polite. What a lovely man he is! I'm so glad we're friends. Her thoughts surprised her. Perhaps it was because for weeks she had not given much thought at all to their relationship.

She had simply drifted along, happy in her new-found confidence. She was seeing quite a lot of James Woodward, who had returned to Peckhurst after going home for a short stay when he had recovered sufficiently from his malaria attack. It was clear to everyone that he was keen on Toni, but she, though enjoying his company, kept him at arm's length, making it plain that she was only interested in the mildest of flirtations. Surprisingly, he seemed not to mind this, apparently getting his kicks out of escorting her around and about. It was a friendship that suited them both.

Of course, Rupert was always there. There were very few days that they didn't meet, either at work or at the tennis club. But quite suddenly Toni realised that they hadn't been alone together since leaving the tennis court that glorious June evening, and she was unhappy about the fact. She swallowed a lump in her throat, and frowned at the idea that he might be avoiding her, or rather be avoiding being alone with her.

What nonsense, I doubt that he's given it a thought, she told herself, and raised her eyes to meet his as he handed her the treatment card on which he had scribbled 'Variclene'.

Their hands touched as she took it from him, and she was aware of a tremor running up her arm as if she had experienced an electric shock. The fine blonde silky hairs on her forearms rose, her hand trembled, and there was a breathless silence.

Rupert stared at her and a variety of expressions

flitted across his face. His eyes darkened. 'Antonia,' he murmured thickly.

Mrs Jackson was speaking. Toni tore her gaze away from his. 'Yes, of course, I'll explain about that, Mrs Jackson.' She produced a smile for the patient and moved towards the couch, hearing as she did so Rupert breathing heavily.

He said in a voice that struggled to be normal, 'I'm going back to my room, Nurse. See you presently when you've finished here.'

Toni dared not look at him again. 'Yes, all right, Doctor.' Resolutely she bent over the patient. 'Now, Mrs Jackson, I'll explain what I'm going to do.'

It took her a quarter of an hour to treat the ulcer and explain to Mrs Jackson how she could bath without getting the dressing wet, by covering her foot and ankle with a plastic bag. 'I'll also give you a waterproof pad to put over it, before you put the bag on,' she said patiently. 'But if you're in doubt, have a shower instead of a bath, and stick your leg outside the curtains.'

Mrs Jackson giggled and said she would try that, though how she would stand on one leg she didn't know.

You could sit down,' suggested Toni. 'Use an old wooden chair or a kitchen stool.'

'Well, I never thought of that,' said Mrs Jackson. 'Aren't you clever?'

At last she was gone, and Toni set about clearing up the clinic-room. Evening surgery was just beginning, so all sorts of sounds were seeping through from outside. Rupert didn't have a surgery that evening. Normally on a Wednesday he and she would go their separate ways until they they met up for a match or practice at the club later.

But she was only too well aware that this was not a normal Wednesday. It was odd—she was tingling with anticipation, breathless with excitement. Her heart thumped, her pulses bounded. She longed to see Rupert, and yet in a most absurd fashion she felt shy about seeing him after the episode in the clinic-room. It was almost as if she were seeing him for the first time.

Surely something tremendous had happened? Her imagination and her natural reserve were beginning to work overtime. Had she only invented the thrill that had surrounded their hand-touching? Was it only she who had been affected by it? No, Rupert had experienced it too. His eyes had revealed so much, they had been full of—what? Compassion, understanding? And his voice, it had surely throbbed with passion, not just desire?

In that instant she knew that what she had experienced had been love. Love, the emotion she'd thought was out of her reach for so long. Had Rupert experienced that too? Love, the willingness to surrender heart, mind and body to someone else, that had seemed an impossible dream, since she had been rejected by her fiancé.

Well, it had taken nearly a year to heal the physical and emotional hurt. Rupert, the gentle physician, the kind man, had started the process when he had walked into her life in the seed house at the nursery, and he'd continued it ever since, taking her hand, metaphorically, and sometimes literally, when she most needed it. He had steered and guided her through a return to normality, unobtrusively, lovingly, without making demands in return.

Most remarkable, of course, was that he had done this without knowing why she had her various hang-ups. Being a doctor, he might have made a guess or two, but he couldn't know the whole. In all fairness, the first thing she must do was tell him everything. The idea was a relief, and rather scary, but something that must be done. She would tell him tonight.

The intercom phone jangled noisily. Like an automaton, she picked it up.

'Antonia, I have to go up to town,' said Rupert's voice in her ear, sounding flat, expressionless.

Toni held the receiver in numb fingers. 'Surely——' she started to say, then stopped.

'I must go, my dear, I simply must. I don't know what time I'll be back. May I ring you, whatever the time?'

'I'm not sure.' She was confused, completely baffled by this latest development, terribly disappointed that she wouldn't be seeing him after the brave plans she'd made. 'How late do you mean?'

'I just don't know. There's a crisis at home. Sophie phoned—my mother's not well. Not terribly serious, I gather, but she wants to see me, and I feel I must go. She's got a slight heart condition and it makes her a bit edgy at times. Antonia, please let me talk to you later.' There was a quality in his voice that she'd never heard before. She wanted to respond to it—it was special.

'All right, I'll turn Grandpa's bedroom phone off so that he isn't disturbed. I do hope your mother isn't too poorly.'

'Oh, I'm sure she isn't, a mild angina probably, but I don't want Sophie to be worried. She has enough on her plate with the new baby.' Rupert sounded rather cross, impatient. Then softly he said, 'Bless you, for agreeing to let me phone later.' He seemed reluctant to put down the phone and Toni guessed he wanted to say more, but after a short silence he simply said, 'Goodbye,' and rang off.

She looked out over the car park and saw him leave a few minutes later. The late afternoon sun was streaming in through the car windows, burnishing his chestnut hair to a coppery red. As if he knew she would be at the clinic window, he turned and raised a hand as he saw her there.

Toni waved in return and impulsively blew him a kiss. He smiled and touched his fingers to his lips in response, then tooted his horn and pulled out into the busy High Street. He was soon out of sight on his way to Dorking.

CHAPTER ELEVEN

IT SEEMED to Toni that time was suspended while she waited for Rupert to phone.

She finished work at the Clinic as soon as possible and was home by just after six. Her grandfather was pleased to see her and learn that she would be having supper with him that evening, something she had seldom done of late.

After supper they wandered down to the glasshouses and potting sheds, with Toni taking the mobile phone with her in case Rupert should ring while she was out of the house.

The brigadier was walking so much better now that his ulcer had healed and he was generally fitter. Something else they owed to Rupert, thought Toni. Her grandfather must have been thinking the same thing, for he stopped in the middle of the drive, waved his stick in the air, and asked, 'How's young Devenish these days? Haven't seen much of him since m'leg improved. Got him to thank for that. Clever young chap. Good job Morris had the sense to let him deal with that blasted ulcer of mine.'

It pleased Toni no end to hear her grandfather praise Rupert. She almost told him how things were shaping up between them, and that they might well become more than good friends, but, since this was based on the fragile exchange this afternoon, she contented herself with explaining how busy he was.

'You know Rupert and I are in the mixed doubles, Grandpa? Well, what with that and his work here and in London, he doesn't have much time for socialising.' On an inspiration she added, 'But I'm sure he'd like to call in some time. Perhaps he'll manage to do that soon.' It seemed an ideal suggestion to pave the way for future confidences.

'Hrrumph.' replied Grandpa gruffly. 'Pleased to see him any time. Good family, y'know. Knew his father. Of course, I've told you that. Horace—Orrie, he was nicknamed, rather younger than I—came through the war all right, then bought it in Northern Ireland in the early seventies. Title went to his elder son, of course, not your young Devenish.'

Toni liked the sound of that 'your young Devenish'. It was strange how her grandfather's conversation was full of Rupert this evening. Almost as if he sensed that something extraordinary had occurred. She looked at the mobile phone and willed it to ring, and for the caller to be Rupert.

It was nearly midnight and she was ambling round her room in a distracted fashion when at last he rang.

Because he had virtually filled her thoughts all the evening, and she had hugged to herself their brief, intimate exchange of the afternoon, she somehow expected him to sound different. Quite how, she wasn't sure, but different. As if the tone of his voice alone would fill in the gaps. In fact, he sounded quite normal, his deep, slightly drawling voice unchanged.

'Antonia, my dear girl, I'm so sorry to be this late. Had rather a busy evening.'

'It's perfectly all right.' Her voice was as normal as his. 'How's your mother?'

'Not too good, actually. She's had a really bad go of angina and has been admitted to the Clinic.'

'I'm so sorry.' It seemed inadequate, but she didn't know what else to say. He had seldom spoken of his mother or his sister-in-law Sophie. She wasn't even sure how close he was to them, apart from the usual duty ties. 'Are you back in Peckhurst?'

'No, I'm staying over for tonight and possibly tomorrow. I'll let you know, of course.'

The 'of course' was some comfort, implying that he wanted to keep in touch on a personal level.

'What about your surgery?'

'I'll phone Morris first thing in the morning; he and the others will have to cover it. Fortunately, with holidays in full force, there'll probably be fewer patients.'

'Oh, yes,' Toni confirmed. 'Fewer patients. Everyone seems to get better at holiday time.'

'Yes.' There was a long pause and she didn't know whether to break into it, or what to say if she did. It was dreadful, this stilted clinical conversation, when all she wanted to hear was. . .

'Antonia, darling,' Rupert's voice was different now, a decibel deeper, a velvety purr, 'I particularly wanted to see you tonight, so that we could talk.' He stopped, and she could hear him clearing his throat. It had returned to its normal drawl when he started speaking again. 'I think it's time we got to know each other better, don't you, dear girl?'

Her heart did acrobatics and her voice wouldn't come forth, even in a squeak.

'Antonia?'

'R-Rupert?' She got it out at last with a stammer and in a whisper. He had called her 'darling' and 'dear girl' as if he meant it.

'Do you agree?'

'Of course I agree.'

'That's marvellous. You are quite sure? What about young Woodward? You and he are pretty thick and seem to enjoy each other's company.'

'I don't belong to James, and why shouldn't I enjoy your company as much as his?'

'Well, I might bore you. He's years younger.'

She said indignantly, 'Why do you always pretend to be so old?'

'Because I'm thirty-eight, and when I look at you and your friends you all look so terribly young and untouched, at the beginning of things. It makes me feel incredibly staid and set in my ways.'

'That's rubbish, ridiculous. You're fitter than nearly everyone else at the club, and you know it.'

Rupert had the grace to laugh at that, and sound apologetic. 'Well, perhaps you're right, and I am in pretty good nick, but I honestly wondered if I'd ever stand a chance with you, dear girl, until this afternoon in the Clinic. Up to now you've always signalled "hands off", so to speak, and I couldn't be sure whether it was just for me or men in general?' There was a question in his voice.

Of course, he must have heard rumours about her. Kieron had said when they first met again that she had a reputation for being an ice maiden, untouchable. Perhaps it was just that, or perhaps he'd heard something more specific?

For the first time since their encounter that afternoon, the feeling that life was wonderful, and all would be well, faded away. At a stroke, cynicism took over. She had been living in a fool's paradise. How could she have thought what had happened to her in the past didn't matter, that he wouldn't mind? It was so odd that the idea hadn't occurred to her. It was as if he must know everything about her. As if the encounter this afternoon had made him aware of what had happened to her. But of course, it hadn't. And when she told him, when he knew?

'There's something you've got to know about me,' she said, her voice trembling. 'But I can't tell you now, over the phone.'

Rupert's voice spoke quietly in her ear. 'Antonia, my dearest, darling girl, I don't know any details, but

I do know that something earth-shattering happened to you not too long ago. Whatever it was, *whatever*,' he insisted, 'it makes no difference, and will never make any difference to the way I feel.'

And how do you feel? she wanted to ask. You haven't actually said. Perhaps what happened this afternoon wasn't significant to you. It was just a sophisticated way of flirting. After all, you're a mature and sophisticated man, a consultant, a VIP in medical circles. Why should you be seriously interested in me?

He was talking about friendship and understanding, but she had ceased to listen properly.

So insistent were her thoughts about his motives that she didn't hear much of what he said. It was dreadful to be relieved when the phone call that she so longed for came to an end.

The next morning the Health Centre, behind the scenes, was like a madhouse. Not only was Rupert absent but Pat MacNiece arrived late. She had been delayed by an early morning visit, tripped over a toy bus that a child had abandoned in the doorway, and fallen, injuring an arm and wrist.

She refused to go to hospital for an X-ray, at least till after surgery. In the absence of an X-ray, Dr Meredith treated the injury as a severe sprain and pulled muscles or ligaments. He immobilised her arm and wrist with a bandage and sling, gave her two Synflex tablets to ease the pain, and reluctantly agreed to her returning to work.

Nearly half an hour had been lost by both doctors, though Frank Morgan had made great inroads into his patients, and offered to start on Rupert's list. It was agreed that Toni should assist Pat when necessary, helping her with examinations and writing up her notes. Fortunately she had only two early bloods booked in, and the receptionist was asked to try to contact later bookings and postpone them.

At least poor Pat's injuries put such pressure of work on Toni that she hadn't time to think about Rupert. Even in the afternoon, when she acted as chauffeur to Pat, driving her to visit a few special patients, she was busy assisting in each house. Only once did the doctor go in to see somebody on her own on a strictly confidential medical matter where Toni's presence wuld have been an embarrassment.

She had ten minutes then to relax and think about Rupert. She longed to see him, to feel his arms about her and his lips on hers. Everything she thought and felt was quite normal. There was nothing ice-maiden-ish about her thoughts. They were exactly what any young woman might indulge in about her lover, except that in her case they couldn't come true.

She must tell Rupert some time what had happened to make her withdrawn and wimpish, and then have the courage to accept his rejection of her. He wouldn't be brash or unkind as Patrick had been, quite the opposite. In fact, she would have to guard against him suggesting that they continue with a relationship, just out of kindness.

She shuddered. She couldn't bear that. To have Rupert appear loving, loverlike, if that was his inten-tion, and yet be inwardly repulsed by any intimacy with her. No, never, she would die rather.

Well, at least she had a few days to come to terms with the situation before seeing him face to face. She could always pretend over the phone.

When Rupert phoned that evening, it was to say that he would be back in Peckhurst the day after tomorrow, Saturday some time, but he didn't know when. His mother was coming home from the Clinic and he wanted to see her installed comfortably before leaving.

'I'm getting a nurse in to keep an eye on her for a bit, which should take care of any future minor emergencies,' he said, his voice sounding rather detached, almost uninterested. And then, taking her by surprise, he asked, 'Are you looking forward to my return, Antonia?'

'Yes, of course I am,' she replied quickly—too quickly perhaps.

'Ah,' he said. 'Fresh doubts about furthering our friendship? Pity. I thought we'd made a good start. I rather thought the old adage about absence making the heart grow fonder might have helped. Still, not to worry, we can maintain the status quo, if you'd rather. Perhaps that would be a sensible thing to do. Goodnight, my dear.' He put the receiver down.

Briefly, Toni was angered by his coolness, but honesty made her admit that it was she who had first retreated from the situation. Why shouldn't he?

It was a great relief to be busy both on duty and off. With the tennis championships looming, she felt compelled to appear at the club for practice, even though Rupert was away. It suited her. She just wanted to keep busy at all times, and shelve her uncomfortable thoughts.

Terry Banks arranged for her to play with several other partners during Rupert's absence, and she worked most of them to death, not sparing herself or them. She played ferociously, hard enough for two, and still missed Rupert's swift movements about the court and their harmonious interplay.

Well, whatever else happens, she thought, returning exhausted to the terrace after a gruelling match on Friday evening, Rupert and I make an almost unbeatable pair on court.

'Come and sit here,' commanded Bridget, patting

the seat beside her. 'I've got you a drink, a lime shandy, stacks of ice—very refreshing.'

'Thanks.' Toni sat down and took a long swig of her drink. 'Great,' she said, wiping her mouth with the back of her hand, and wondering how quickly she could leave without causing comment, or having to enter into conversation about Rupert.

It was the latter that she dreaded most. Bridget knew her so well and would soon cotton on to the fact that something was amiss between her and Rupert, even though she hadn't been aware of the latest situation between them.

The notion floated through Toni's mind that she might confide something of her fears to Bridget. Why not? Her old friend was one of the few people here who knew what had happened to her in London. She was discretion itself when necessary, and she might, just might be able to suggest how Toni put Rupert in the picture without irrevocably spoiling things between them.

Beneath the bubbly, rather fluffy surface Bridget was a kind and very practical person. Perhaps talking to her would be a good idea.

In the end, Toni didn't have to make a decision. James Woodward, who was staying at the Mariner's Arms since his return to Peckhurst, appeared on the terrace and spotted Toni and Bridget at once.

'May I join you?' he asked, and, though he included them both, his eyes were on Toni. Bridget wondered just how keen he was on her friend, and if he were responsible for the bleak look that had reappeared in Toni's eyes.

'Yes, of course. Do sit here,' replied Toni with a smile. She pulled forward a chair and made ample room beside her.

Bridget noticed, though, that it was quite an ordinary social smile that she gave him, and concluded that James was not responsible for Toni's withdrawn expression. To her way of thinking, this left only one contender in the field, and he was away at present.

'I believe Rupert's returning tomorrow,' she announced out of the blue, and noted with interest that Toni blushed and paled at the mention of his name.

'Yes,' said Toni in as casual a tone as she could muster. 'Dr Meredith said he'd be back then. It'll be a great relief all round, for although the surgeries are less full with ordinary patients in the holiday season there are lots of temporary residents who come to the Health Centre.'

As she said it, she knew it was a ridiculous thing to say. Bridget knew the situation better than she herself did, and James hadn't a clue about the comings and goings of patients, and couldn't care less.

She kept her head bent over her drink and felt, rather than saw the penetrating look her friend gave her. Almost certainly Bridget had guessed about herself and Rupert, and suspected that there was more to their relationship than being just tennis partners. Well, perhaps she would swallow her pride and her natural reticence and confide in her some time.

James was rattling on about the forthcoming tournament. 'I'm looking forward to it very much,' he said. 'From what everyone says the mixed doubles final should be terrific. But then look who's playing,' he touched Toni lightly on the arm. 'She's not only a great nurse, but some sharp lady on the court. That service!' He raised his eyes heavenward.

Toni tried to join in the usual lightweight banter that was exchanged between club members, but after a while she announced that she was going.

Bridget decided to leave with her, and they walked together to the car park. Toni was glad of her company, for James had been difficult to shake off, and, even though she thought he now had the message, she was rather afraid he might follow her to her car if she was on her own.

It meant, of course, that she and Bridget were alone for the first time that evening, and, as she'd suspected, Bridget was curious, if in a kindly fashion, about her relationship with Rupert.

'Are you all right, Toni?' she asked, her voice concerned. 'You look. . .' She hesitated. 'You look a bit bothered. Man trouble?'

Toni forced a laugh. 'You could say that.'

'I honestly don't want to pry, but if it's any help I'm around to talk to.'

'Yes, thanks, I know.' Toni flung her gear into the back seat of the Land Rover. 'It's just that I. . .' She couldn't bring herself to say more.

'I'll hazard a guess,' said Bridget. 'You don't know how much to tell him, right?'

'Right.'

'And it is Rupert Devenish?'

'Yes.'

'Why don't you tell him every little thing. He's above average, that guy, both as a man and a medic. I doubt you'll take him by surprise.'

'Do you know something that I don't, for instance, that he already knows about me?'

'No.' Bridget gave her a sly grin and put on the Irish accent that occasionally surfaced. 'But to be sure now, and he's a lovely man altogether, he'll understand. Just give him the chance, Toni.'

'I don't know if I've got the nerve. Do you see, he might be too good? I c-couldn't bear it if he,' Toni's voice dropped to an agonised whisper, 'if he was just sorry for me. I'd rather we just stayed as we are.'

Bridget stared at her friend. 'I don't think that'll work forever,' she said at last. 'He wouldn't stand for it, and it wouldn't be fair to expect it of him. He's male, fit and mad for you, I should think.' Suddenly she was intense. 'Toni, don't drive him away. Let him decide. If he really loves you, it'll come out right.'

Rupert phoned Toni at the Health Centre the next morning. 'I'll be back late afternoon,' he said sounding quite brisk and businesslike, perhaps because he thought the receptionist might still be linked to the extension. 'We'd better try to get in a practice match. Will you fix a court, Antonia?'

'Yes, of course. Terry's provisionally set us one aside for six-thirty, that should give us about an hour and a half of good light. He's trying to make sure that all the match players get in some practice before play starts in earnest on Sunday.'

'Splendid—I'll make it by then. Suppose I pick you up from Timbers at about six o'clock?'

'Lovely. See you then. It'll give you time to say a quick hello to Grandpa. He was saying he'd seen very little of you lately.'

'No, don't promise him I'll see him tonight, we'll only just make it to the club, and I'm not sure about later.'

'Oh, all right. See you at six.' Slowly Toni put down the phone and stared blankly round the clinic-room. How strange and distant he'd sounded. But why shouldn't he? she reminded herself. She'd not exactly been bubbling over with enthusiasm. She knew, though, why she was cool to the point of seeming indifferent, but what excuse had he?

Mechanically she tidied up the room. There was nothing else for her to do, as the surgery closed at eleven on a Saturday. No more patients were waiting. She heard the receptionist go through to the cloak-room, and then Dr Meredith, who had been on duty, popped his head round the door.

'I'm off now, Toni, all seems to be reasonably quiet. Tell your grandfather I'll be up this evening.'

'Right, will do.'

The elderly doctor came further into the room. 'Are you all right?' he asked, looking intently at her.

'I'm fine, Uncle Morris, fine.'

'You look a bit pale.'

'That's working for you, you're such a slavedriver.' She managed a laugh.

'Well, keep yourself fit enough to win those championships,' he told her. 'I'm depending on you and young Devenish. By the way, he phoned just now, and he'll be back this evening.' He gave her a knowing sort of look. 'Of course, you probably know that already. I dare say he phoned you, yes?'

Again Toni smiled. 'Yes, we've got a practice on tonight.'

'Jolly good. See you then.'

She waited in front of the house for Rupert to arrive, plucking the odd weed from the flower-filled beds that bordered the wide sweep of gravel drive, her tummy churning with anticipation. She longed to see him, but what did she expect from him, what would she say to him? How would he greet her? How would she respond? Nothing was resolved.

She was dressed ready for tennis practice, in brief white shorts and a sensible Aertex shirt blocked out in blue and white. The plain clean lines of her clothes emphasised her cool flaxen beauty, boyish athletic figure and golden tan.

She heard the car turn into the drive, then he was there.

'You look gorgeous, definitely edible,' he said with a laugh as he got out of the car and strode towards her. He was so loving and exuberant that in spite of her reservations, she fell helplessly into his arms. He bent his head and kissed her passionately, longingly, his self-imposed guard lowered. Hungrily, amazingly, Toni kissed him back, standing in front of the blazing bed of blue delphiniums, dusky lupins and smouldering red salvias.

'Hello.' He smiled down at her, his eyes dark with what. . .love, desire? A desire held in strict control? His long, lean face was creased into a rueful smile. He eased his arms that were holding her tightly. 'I must apologise for ringing off so abruptly on Thursday. Will you accept that I'd had one of those days?'

'Yes, of course—certainly,' she confirmed in a cool voice, wishing she hadn't responded so readily to his kiss. They both knew he had rung off because of her coldness, her uncertainty.

'Thanks.' He shrugged expressively. 'We seem to have problems at the moment, but surely nothing that can't be resolved, given time?' He was suddenly fierce—hopeful! He squeezed her arm so hard that it hurt.

'Yes, perhaps.' Toni dared not go further.

Rupert let go of her arm. 'We'd better get going, then. We need this practice match.' His voice was remote, barely friendly.

'Yes. Would you mind if I take the Land Rover?' she asked politely. 'Just in case either of us wants to leave the club at a different time?'

'No, not at all—good idea. I've offered to be on call from midnight. Least I could do after being absent half the week.'

So, she thought much later as she drove herself home, you've managed this evening without having to face up to the situation. Coward!

It was several days later, and they were well into a week of eliminating matches, when Rupert drove Toni back to Timbers from the club. They'd had a really busy day at the Health Centre. In fact they'd had many busy days, making it easy for them to avoid being alone together, until tonight.

However, avoiding him had still been an exhausting business. Maintaining a sort of affectionate camaraderie in front of other people was a chastening experience. Toni had no way of knowing if Rupert felt the same. Over the last few days, both at work and at the club, they had touched and parted on the most superficial level.

He had not referred to her reaction to him when he had returned on Saturday night. He remained aloof. When they met or parted, he sometimes brushed her cheek with an apology of a kiss. It seemed that this restrained behaviour suited him as well as it at present suited her. Probably he had his own secret reasons for not pursuing a more positive course of action. Would she ever know what they were?

He never alluded to that moment of magic that Wednesday afternoon in the clinic, or to his insistence over the phone that nothing she had to declare would make any difference to his attitude towards her. Apparently he was for the moment content to take his cue from her and play down the love angle.

But his equanimity made it no easier for Toni to decide whether or not to confess everything to him and hope he would either reject her flat out, or accept her as she was, a flawed human being.

Stop it! she told herself. Stop imagining scenarios. Do it, or don't do it. But make up your mind whether you're going to do it now, or never.

Rupert was holding open the car door. 'Come on, Antonia, snap out of it,' he said in an even, cheerful voice; but when she looked up to give him an apologetic smile, she could see, by the faint light of the moon, that he was looking down at her intently. Surely he couldn't know she had reached a momentous decision?

She gave him her hand, and felt the familiar thrill as he took it and pulled her gently from the car. 'R-Rupert, there's something I must tell you.' To her surprise, her voice came out firmly, except for the slight stammer. She drew in a deep breath. 'I——'

Before she could say more, the heavy front door was flung open and light streamed out from the wide hall. The brigadier stood silhouetted in the light. His parade-ground voice boomed out. 'Thought it was the pair of you. Call for you, Devenish, put through from the answer service. They want you to phone back pronto.'

'Thank you, sir,' said Rupert, and muttered something under his breath. 'My mobile phone seems to be on the blink. May I use yours?'

'Certainly you may.' The brigadier stumped his way back into the hall.

Rupert squeezed Toni's arm as they walked across the gravel to the front door. 'Sorry about this,' he said. 'It may be a call out, though I'm not officially on for another hour. If I've got to rush off now, I won't see you till Friday evening when I'll be back in time for the semi-finals. As you know, I'm in London all day tomorrow and most of Friday. Hold on to whatever it was that you wanted to tell me. Don't be afraid— anticipation is worse than the telling. Perhaps everything will come right between us, who knows?'

He turned her to him, put a hand beneath her chin and tipped her face up to meet his. 'I've been wanting to do this again for a long time,' he murmured, and covered her mouth with his in a firm, at first gentle kiss, but a kiss that suddenly flared into passion. 'Don't forget that,' he said in a matter-of-fact voice, 'when you're wondering in the small hours whether you want to tell me whatever it is that's bothering you.'

Then, with the ability he had of becoming professional to the exclusion of all else, he released her and strode into the hall, making straight for the telephone. 'Now, let's find out what this call is all about,' he said, and dialled a number.

It was an emergency, and he left immediately, after thanking the brigadier for the use of the phone, and wishing Toni a quiet goodnight.

Later, Toni thought about what he had said, and the way he had said it. He had been so calm, so strong. It was almost as if he knew what she was going to tell him, and didn't care a jot.

There was no question now in her mind about telling him. She had screwed up her courage that one night, and knew she could do it again, but it had to be the right moment. Somehow that had become as important as what she had to say, because she had to judge Rupert's reaction correctly. Her worst fear remained, that he would stick by her out of kindness, and more than ever now she knew that it was total trust and warm, passionate love that she wanted from him. Anything else would be unthinkable.

CHAPTER TWELVE

TONI went to work the next afternoon feeling calm and collected for the first time in days. Coming so near to telling Rupert everything last night, and his sensible words about trusting him when he had been compelled to rush off, had brought her to her senses and restored her courage.

He wouldn't reject her out of hand, or pretend to an affection that wasn't genuine. He knew that something unpleasant had happened to her, and even when she revealed what that squalid something was he wouldn't be shocked into acting as her unspeakable fiancé had. If, after he had heard her story, he was prepared to love her, then she must be prepared to accept that that was what he meant. She must trust his judgement utterly.

By the time she reached the Health Centre, much comforted by her thoughts of Rupert, she was in an elated mood. She hardly noticed the humid sticky heat, or the leaden grey skies tinted with yellow ochre, or the occasional gust of wind that stirred up the dust and bowled shreds of paper and leaves before it.

Tomorrow night she would see Rupert and tell him everything after they had won the semi-finals, and such was her present confidence that she had no doubt they would win. A perfect partnership both on and off court, she thought, and suppressed a giggle as she passed a patient in the entrance.

She made for the clinic-room. There were two ECGs to do, stitches to remove from a foot wound, and a prophylactic injection, the last in a current series to give to a long-suffering hay fever patient. After that she would get ready for the Well Woman Clinic, programmed from five-thirty to seven-thirty.

Even though there were fewer women than usual at the clinic on account of its being holiday time, it was nearly eight o'clock before she finished.

The weather had greatly deteriorated since she had come on duty, and the rain was now bucketing down. Holding her anorak over her head, Toni bolted for her car, suddenly conscious of how cold it was.

'You'd never believe it was August,' shouted one of the community nurses, as they battled against the elements. 'More like December. Morton's Bridge by the dip is flooded.'

'Right, thanks for telling me,' Toni yelled over the noise of the rain drumming down on the car roof. 'I'll go over the hill.'

She started up the chalky lane in her little yellow Mini. She preferred the rather dilapidated Land Rover, but today Felicity was using that at the nursery, hence the Mini.

It happily negotiated the steeply sloping lane, wet and slippery though it was. 'You beauty,' said Toni, patting the dashboard as she made the final turn to the top of the hill. The lane here was really little more than a track running along the side of the hill, and used by vehicles from Tophill Farm when ploughing the high meadows or muck-spreading.

It was still called Windmill Hill, though the windmill, bereft of sails and its brickwork crumbling for many years, was barely visible—just a mouldering heap of bricks on the highest point of the hill, almost buried beneath a rambling growth of brambles and nettles, with a barbed-wire fence erected around it to keep out the sheep that were occasionally grazed on that part of the downs. Children from Washbourne village sometimes went up there to play, or pick blackberries, ignoring the notices warning of crumbling walls.

The rain which had drenched her in the valley had almost stopped, but she was now driving into low cloud, which was saturating the air with moisture in a thick fog. A fog that billowed and swirled as the intermittent wind moved it, opening up occasional tunnels of visibility, and then closing again within a short distance.

On an ordinary evening there would still have been some daylight left, but the lowering clouds and fog had turned everything into night.

Toni switched on her fog lamps and peered between the swishing blades of the window wipers, edging along at a snail's pace following the tiny arc of light from the lamps. A gust of wind parted the veil for a moment, and she spurted forward as fast as she dared, until she was shrouded in fog again.

The windows misted up inside and out, despite the warm air pulsing out from the heater. The track was invisible, and she dared not move. She wiped the windows with a cloth and peered ahead. She was about halfway along the ridge. Was it worth trying to reach the far side of the hill where the lane descended sharply to Washbourne and Timbers? Perhaps the fog hadn't reached the valley; it could be clear there.

Should she sit and wait for the fog to lift, or continue her crawling journey and risk getting stuck? Or should she try walking the half-mile or so along the ridge to the lane?

She would walk. She had a powerful torch, a plastic mac to put over her summer-weight anorak, and an umbrella providentially discovered on the back seat. Her soft black leather duty shoes weren't made for rough walking, but were all she had. If she'd been driving the Land Rover she would have had wellies in the back. But then she wouldn't be here at all; she'd have risked the other route home and made it through the water at Morton's Bridge.

Before setting out, she put the car into reverse gear, turned on the flashers in addition to the fog lamps and set the emergency flashing light on the car roof. She switched off the engine, but left the ignition on, lights blazing, and radio turned up full blast. If she got out of range of the lights, she might still be able to hear the radio and get back to the car if necessary.

Knowing the terrain, she made good progress. She could still see the muted flashes of light coming from the Mini, and hear the occasional crashing chords of Beethoven's Fifth, da-da-da-*da*, da-da-da-*da*, when she drew level with the crumbling remains of the windmill. Now she knew exactly where she was. A few yards ahead the track would turn round the curve of the hill, and the lane to the village and home would lie only a few hundred yards beyond that.

'Great,' she said, and her voice floated disembodied in the fog-shrouded landscape. She flashed her torch over the heap of bricks that was all that was left of the windmill that gave the hill its name. It was dealthy quiet.

She stood on the slippery, chalky track and shivered from cold—she was beaded with icy drops of water— and from a 'someone walked over my grave' sensation—terrifying. Her high spirits plummeted. The flashing car lights had disappeared, and even Beethoven at his thunderous best had wavered into nothingness. . .then eerily, into this quiet, grey nothingness, a sound penetrated. An animal or a human sound? It was coming from the ruins.

Toni listened intently. It sounded like a sneeze, a sneeze muffled by the fog.

A child, she thought, a kid caught up here in the dark. 'It's all right, I'm coming,' she shouted, but even to herself the words sounded muted. 'I'm coming,' she shouted again, louder, and scrambled over the muddy ground beside the track.

The barbed wire had been wrenched apart. She crouched and eased herself through the narrow space. Her coronet of hair got tangled in the wire above her, and she pulled it free, hardly noticing the pain as strands of hair were pulled from her scalp.

The creature, child, whatever, sneezed again, a loud, crashing sneeze followed by a thunderous bellow. Toni stopped a few feet from the broken-down entrance. Her skin crawled, hair stood up on the back of her neck. It was a man's voice that she could hear, not a child's cry, not a domestic animal's bleat or moo or bark, but a man's voice, furious, roaring, explosive, giving vent to uncontrollable rage.

She froze. Only once before had she felt so alone, so vulnerable. Then a man had jumped out of the bushes in the wet darkness of the night, and. . . Hands all over her, tearing at clothes and hair, beery breath, a hand clamping her mouth. Something gleaming in the other hand—a scalpel. On the ground, a bulky shape pressing on her, a voice she recognised, angry, accusing. 'Icy bitch!' Her own voice trembling, 'Tim!' A frenzy of words pouring from him as he ripped at her clothes and reached her body. 'Adored you, afraid to touch you. . .even your precious Patrick. . .softly, softly. . .everyone knows.' Wanting to cover her ears, fighting to be calm. . .keep talking, not. . .hurting. . . not. . .begging. . .'Stop—please stop!' Later, much later, blood, wet, mud, sore lips, dull pain, dulled senses, ashamed, unseen stumbling back to the nurses' home. Showers, baths, over and over, wash it away . . .away.

Toni gritted her teeth. The memory of that night had flashed through her mind in seconds. She pushed it aside and called up all her reserves of courage. Whoever was in the ruins might need help. She couldn't pass by; training and humanity demanded that she should investigate. No way could she leave someone, perhaps in trouble, to fend for themselves, not even an angry, potentially threatening man.

It was at this moment, when Toni stood terrified but determined on the rough footpath heading for the ruins, that Rupert arrived in Peckhurst, and went straight to the Health Centre.

'Is Antonia here?' he asked Laura Lacy, the receptionist, who was about to lock up.

'Oh, no, Doctor, she left about a quarter of an hour ago.'

'I heard that the road to Washbourne was flooded. Is that right?'

'Yes. Toni probably went over the hill, or the long way round through Ditchmouth.'

'How long would the Ditchmouth route take her?' asked Rupert.

'Half an hour, forty minutes perhaps.'

'And over the hill?'

'About twenty minutes normally,' said Laura.

'Do you mean the rain might slow her down?'

'That and the fog. Mr Legget from Tophill Farm was in earlier, he reckons the track's like a sleigh run, very slippery on account of the wet chalk, and the hill's covered in low cloud, fog really, almost nil visibility.'

'Do you think it's likely that Antonia went that way, rather than the other?' asked Rupert.

'Probably. She mightn't have known about the fog when she left, and she knows the track well.'

At that moment the phone rang, and, after announcing the surgery, Laura listened before quickly handing the receiver to Rupert. 'It's the police.'

Rupert looked his surprise as he took the phone from Laura. 'Devenish speaking.'

'We have a problem, Doctor. Legget of Tophill Farm reported rustlers, and we arrived in the middle of their endeavours. We've got all of those involved, except a younger man who legged it across the fields, towards the old windmill, we think. We know he's armed, but in this weather he shouldn't meet anyone. If he does, or if he gets himself into trouble, we're likely to need your services, and we wanted you to be on standby, just in case.'

Already worried about Toni, Rupert listened with increasing anxiety before rapidly explaining his concerns about Toni's possible route home. Arranging to meet the police at the windmill, Rupert turned and left the building, running with long strides back to his car. Laura watched him start up his new Range Rover, race out of the car park, and turn left to head up the hill.

Toni approached the ruins cautiously. The voice was still carrying on swearing and cursing, but now that she was nearby she could make out exclamations of pain mingling with the stream of blasphemy. It was probably an old tramp sheltering for the night. Well, at least she had nothing to fear; whoever it was was hurt, and would be glad to see help arrive.

She called out again as she reached the mound of bricks and rubble that half filled the door space. Once upon a time the doorway, high in the side of the building, had been approached by half a dozen brick steps. These had long since crumbled and been buried in the rubble from the falling walls of the mill. Now all that was left of the doorway was an aperture at the top of the mound of broken masonry. She shone the torch light up at the gap.

The violent stream of words ceased, and everything went quiet. It was unnerving.

'Hello,' Toni called in a rather shaky voice. 'I've c-come to help.'

The silence persisted. She lowered the torch and shone it on the pile of broken bricks, then started to ascend cautiously. She crouched at the top of the mound and peered through the gap, directing her torch into the inky blackness. Broken bricks and stones formed a rough slope on the inside of the mill.

She could hear heavy, rasping breaths to one side of the broken doorway. Perhaps he wasn't answering because he'd fainted with pain, or was frightened of being found trespassing. She crawled through the small opening and scrambled down to the floor.

'Hello,' she repeated for the umpteenth time. 'Do say something—I only want to help.'

She moved round a heap of broken bricks, where the wall and part of the floor above had collapsed, and flashed the torch around trying to focus on the point where the heavy breathing was coming from. In the wavering light she caught sight of a lumpy form huddled against the wall, and bent towards it. So fast that it made her jump, the torch was snatched from her hand and beamed straight into her eyes.

She gasped with fright, but managed to speak through her fear, controlling her voice, desperately trying to ignore the fact that she couldn't see the man behind the torchlight. 'Are you hurt?' she asked.

'Too bloody right I am,' snarled a voice out of the darkness. 'But don't get any ideas, I'm not bloody helpless. I've got this.' A hand moved into sight holding something that glinted in the beam of light. It was a gun, and it was pointing at her.

Toni breathed in sharply, noisily, and still crouching, scuffled backwards.

'Scared?' taunted the voice, menacingly, then let out another stream of oaths ending with, 'Bloody, flaming leg.'

Whether it was the menace in his voice, or his obvious pain, or because she thought she heard the sound of a vehicle up on the track, Toni didn't know, but she willed herself to speak again, and even move fractionally forward to distract him. 'I'm a nurse,' she said. 'Let me have a look at your leg—perhaps I can help.'

'Did you 'ear something?' He leaned forward and for the first time she glimpsed his face as it moved into the arc of light. Younger than she'd thought, unshaven, frightened, sweaty.

'No.' She shuffled forward a little further. 'Will you let me look at your leg?'

''ow do I know you're a nurse?'

'I've got my uniform dress on.' She undid her mac and her anorak, revealing her navy dress and silver-buckled belt. In an abstracted fashion, she thought, thank God for all the hospital programmes. Nearly everyone recognises the symbols of nursing now.

His face was still visible. He was staring intently at her buckle. 'Yeah,' he said at last, 'you're a nurse. Right, you can 'ave a look at me leg. But remember, I got this.' He waved the gun about, and instinctively she ducked. He laughed, a grating, pain-filled laugh, full of bravado. But bravado or not, he had got a gun.

Everything outside had gone quiet. Had she heard an engine? Was she now imagining stealthy sounds from without? She prayed that whoever it was wouldn't do anything that would alert the man with the gun.

'You'll have to shine the torch on your leg,' she said loudly. 'I can't help you otherwise.' And then, inspired, and even more loudly, 'And please don't wave that gun about, it frightens me.' Would whoever it was outside understand? Would they hear?

Incredibly the gunman seemed apologetic. 'Oh, sorry, Nurse,' he said, as if they were in a hospital ward. He focused the torch on his leg. His denims were encrusted with blood, and there was an ominous-looking spiky lump about halfway up his thigh, pushing against the tight material of his jeans. The material over his calf was torn and a trickle of blood was oozing from it.

Toni stared at the injured leg. 'You need a lot of treatment,' she said. 'You've broken your thigh-bone and probably one of your shin-bones too. You need hospital treatment.'

'No bloody way—you treat it. Bandage it up or something.'

'I can't do that without my first-aid box. That's in the car. Can I fetch it?'

'No, yer bloody can't.'

'I don't know what I can do to help you, then.'

At that moment there was the faintest glimmer of a light in the gap. Toni was aware of it, but willed herself not to look at it. The injured man was still focusing the torch on his leg and seemed mesmerised.

'Can't yer do nothin'?' he asked, his voice edgy with disbelief and pain.

'If you'd let me get my first-aid box I could give you some painkillers, and clean up that cut on your shin, cover it over.'

She raised her voice as a dark form began to lower itself stealthily through the gap, and bent forward until her face was almost meeting that of the injured man. It seemed impossible that he wasn't aware of what was happening a few yards away, even though he was facing her and away from the door, and the partly broken wall almost obscured his line of sight. 'I wish I could do more,' she said.

She was so close that she could smell his sweat and fear. 'I'm so sorry.' She touched his unshaven cheek, suppressing a shudder. She dared not look at the gap to confirm what some sixth sense had already told her, that it was Rupert who was so cautiously entering the mill. Only he would have grasped the situation and acted accordingly; anyone else would have blundered in and made matters worse.

Ridiculously, all she could think of was that Rupert should be in London. He had clinics and lectures and patients to see at his rooms. His being here didn't make sense, but she was glad that he was.

The gunman raised his eyes from his leg, and she could see in the faint light that he was looking at her, but not seeing her. He was frowning, and listening hard—concentrating. The hand holding the gun shook slightly.

She cleared her throat loudly. 'Here,' she said, 'take my anorak—you're cold.' She began struggling with her clothes, moving as noisily as she could, anything to distract him.

The torch went out and clattered on the floor. Her wrist was grasped in a vicelike grip and the gun was pressed hard against her chest. 'You bloody bitch,' grated the gunman's voice in her ear. Then she felt him turn his head as he spoke into the darkness. 'There's a gun in 'er chest, and I'll shoot if yer come any nearer,' he threatened in a hard voice.

Rupert's deep, drawling voice came through the darkness. 'Is it true, Antonia? Is it aimed at you?'

Before she could anser, the gunman ground out, 'You'd better believe it, mate. I gotta gun, and it's pressed against 'er 'eart, give or take an inch.'

For a moment there was silence. Then Rupert asked again in the same unruffled voice, 'Antonia, is this true?'

For the merest fraction of a second, she felt the pressure of the gun's muzzle ease. 'Yes, it's true,' she replied, her voice amazingly steady.

She and the gunman heard Rupert move. The gunman tensed. When next Rupert spoke, it was from the other side of the circular room, a good twenty-five feet away. 'Right, young man,' he said coolly, conversationally. 'Why don't you let Miss King go? I'll stay here. I believe I'm almost opposite you, but you can shine the torch and establish that. Then you can aim at me and you can make sure that the lady moves to the side away from the door, so she can't raise the alarm.'

Toni said in an anguished voice, knowing she was a thousand times more terrified for Rupert than for herself, 'No, Rupert, no. You go, get help—he can't see you. Go, please go.'

The gunman whistled through his teeth. 'So that's the way of it. That's why you came over this godforsaken 'ill. Keepin' tabs on 'er, were you?'

'Something like that.' Rupert sounded weary, bored even, so drawling and laid-back was his tone.

The gunman had courage too, thought Toni. He must be in excruciating pain, yet somehow he kept talking. Perhaps that was a good sign. Weren't hostages supposed to try to get friendly with their captors? The gun was still pressed against her chest and the injured man still held her close with a painful grip, but she was beginning to feel less afraid. She was sure that the longer he could be kept talking, the less likely he would be to pull the trigger.

'Rupert's a doctor,' she said as casually as she could. 'He might be able to help you.'

'Rupert's a doctor,' the man mimicked in a falsetto and over-posh voice. 'Well, *you* couldn't 'elp me, *Nurse*, could yer, so 'ow the 'ell's 'e goin' to? I don't suppose you 'ad the sense to bring your medical bag, did yer, Doc, when yer was chasin' yer girlfriend?' His voice was heavy with sarcasm, and yet Toni fancied there was a note of hope in it.

Rupert's voice, cool and toneless, came out of the darkness. 'Well, no, actually, I don't have it on me, so to speak, but it's in my car up on the track. Only take me a couple of minutes to fetch it.'

'You must think I'm off me trolley if yer think I'm going to let yer out of this 'ell 'ole so yer can get the p'lice and 'alf the bloody Army 'ere.'

'Well, I did think,' said Rupert, his voice mild as milk, 'that as you have my fiancée captive, as it were, you could time me while I fetched the bag. I wouldn't do anything that might harm her—you must see that. It's simple, you hold all the aces. I give you my word I'll come straight back.'

Toni, in spite of the situation, in spite of knowing that Rupert had only referred to her as his fiancée to stengthen his position, still felt a thrill of pride go through her.

The gunman considered what Rupert had said. His grip first tightened and then relaxed on her wrist, and momentarily he lowered the gun, but it was soon back in position. Both his hands and arms must be aching unbearably, she thought, and he must be getting weaker. I wish we could do something about his leg, it's in a dreadful state.

'Do let Rupert go and get his bag,' she pleaded. 'He's given his word he won't try to contact anyone.'

Again the tenseness in the man's fingers that circled her wrist changed. He's going to let Rupert go, she thought, and a wave of relief washed over her. It was weird to feel happy in the circumstances, but she was.

'Give us yer word yer won't do nothing but fetch yer case?'

'Word of honour.'

'OK, Doc, yer on. Two minutes.'

'Three, I need three—it's foggy, slippery, wet.'

'Three, or *Antonia*,' the man tried unsuccessfully to imitate Rupert's cultured drawl, 'gets it.'

The gun was jabbed even harder against her and she gave an involuntary, 'Oh!' of pain.

There was a slight movement from Rupert, and for one dreadful moment Toni thought he was going to attack the man. 'I'm all right,' she called. 'Go, please go.'

She heard him draw in a deep breath. 'Right, I'm going now.' Footsteps crossed the stony floor towards the grey gap at the top of the mound, then she could see the bulk of his body as he climbed out through the doorway and disappeared.

The ruined room seemed colder, emptier, darker once he had gone. Toni shivered. 'I've got cramp,' she said, easing herself from one knee to another.

'Yer can sit,' said the man. He let go of her wrist and picked up the torch and switched it on, shining it as before in her face. The muzzle of the gun was still pressed against her chest. 'No tricks.'

Toni shook her head. 'I promise,' she said, and began slowly to move her legs. It was difficult, slewing them round over the rough ground without getting up, but she didn't dare do anything that might disturb the position of the gun, afraid he would shoot if she did.

She had one leg free, stuck out sideways, but knew she would have to at least raise her buttocks to release the other. 'I have to partly sit up,' she said. The beam of the torch was lowered from her face to the point where the gun rested.

'Right, get on with it.'

Slowly she raised herself, and the man with the gun followed her movements, raising his arm and the weapon as she straightened up. He groaned, then swore. 'Bloody leg, bloody leg.' The pressure on her chest weakened, and suddenly it was gone. The torch swivelled downwards and the beam streamed out over the stony floor. There was a dull thud as the injured man dropped back against the wall and the gun fell from his hand. He had fainted.

It was a moment before Toni realised what had

happened. She freed her other leg, stood up cautiously and retrieved the torch from the floor and shone it on his pale, pain-filled face, and muttered in anguish, 'Oh, no.' Then she remembered the gun and shone the torch around till it lighted on the grey metallic shape. She picked it up and threw it away behind her as far as she could.

Intermittent flashes of light glimmered through the gap, accompanied by the thud of running feet. The light shone full through the broken-down doorway and Rupert's voice, rasping with effort, floated into the mill. 'I'm back, and I've got my bag—I'm pushing that through first, right?'

On stiff legs, Toni walked across to the bottom of the heap of debris. 'It's all right,' she said in a quiet voice, seeing his astonishment as she appeared. 'The poor man's fainted.' She picked up the bag and walked back to the huddled form.

Rupert let himself down through the gap, his torch shining on her back. In two strides he was at her side, his hand on her arm. 'Antonia—dear, darling girl, are you all right?' His voice had lost its laid-back drawl. He sounded uncertain, urgent, loving, as if nothing but her safety was important.

She turned to smile at him in the torchlight, fighting down the desire to throw herself into his arms. 'I'm fine,' she said calmly. 'Fine, but this poor man needs our help.' They had arrived at the side of the injured gunman. He was just beginning to come round. He stared at them both. With the two torches switched on the old ruined room was quite well lit.

His face was waxen pale, glistening with the sweat of pain and fear. 'Bloody 'ell,' he muttered, trying to raise himself up.

'You fainted,' said Toni matter-of-factly, 'while Dr Devenish was fetching his bag.'

All sorts of emotions and thoughts passed across the

man's face. 'Yer didn't cheat, then?' he asked surprisingly, at last.

'No, I promise you we didn't.'

He would have shrugged if he could, but hadn't the strength left. 'Luck of the draw,' he mumbled, and drifted off again into oblivion.

'He needs a shot of morphine,' said Rupert, very much the doctor. 'Draw up fifteen mg, please, the syringes are in the side pocket—oh, and hand me my stethoscope, I'll have a listen to his chest. He sounds very croaky, poor devil. Then we'll see what we can do to make him more comfortable.'

'Yes, sir, certainly, sir,' said Toni with overdone professionalism, and suppressing a giggle. Reaction was making her feel high as a kite, silly and happy and full of love for the man who was kneeling opposite her and concentrating all his skill on the person who had so recently threatened to kill them.

Rupert looked across at her. The light from the torches lit his narrow intelligent face from below and darkened his eyes into violet pools. 'Oh, my darling, I don't mean to order you around, it's just that. . .'

'You're a doctor and I'm a nurse, and where a patient's life is concerned that's how it sometimes has to be. It's the nature of things in our work. Rule one for nurses, "Doctors Maketh Slaves Of Us All", but as long as they're good doctors, we don't mind.'

They eyed each other over the prone figure. Toni held up the syringe and the empty ampoule to show what she'd drawn up. Rupert nodded. 'You give it,' he said, and pulled up the man's sleeve so that she could inject into his forearm.

She swabbed the area with an antiseptic wipe, and said automatically to the somnolent man, 'I'm going to give you a little scratch in your arm. It'll help the pain.'

'We'll give it a moment to work and then do something about this leg,' said Rupert.

'Yes.' They smiled at each other in perfect accord.

Rupert said casually, 'I'd be your slave off duty.'

Toni's usually rather solemn grey eyes sparkled with fun. 'That sounds fair enough,' she said. 'A fifty-fifty division of slaving.'

'I love you, Antonia King,' said Rupert, reverting to his deepest laid-back drawl. 'You're lovely and funny and a wonderful nurse, and you play tennis like an angel. Do you think you could bear to marry me?' He reached down and took the unconscious man's pulse, but his eyes were still on Toni's face.

She said, her eyes still bright with love, her voice little more than a whisper, 'Will you ask me again after I've told you something that I must?'

'Ah, yes,' he said, his wide generous mouth quirked at the corners. 'This world-shattering secret that I've already told you won't make one iota of difference to the way I feel.'

Toni nodded.

'Well, if I must I must,' he conceded. 'But not in here. One proposal's enough in this " 'ell 'ole" as our friend called it. I've somewhere much more suitable in mind.' He leaned down and lifted the gunman's eyelids and examined his eyes with a tiny pencil torch that he unclipped from the top pocket of his elegant suit. 'He's as ready as he'll ever be for us to deal with this leg,' he said. 'We'll have to splint the fractured one to the good leg.'

'We could try using my brolly as an outside splint,' Toni suggested.

'Good thinking, Holmes.'

'No, you're Holmes, you're the leader.'

'No, I'm Watson, I'm only the doctor.'

They grinned at each other like idiots and then set to work on their patient, who in spite of being half drugged, and their being incredibly gentle, moaned occasionally as they dealt with his injured leg.

As always, they worked harmoniously and efficiently together. It was almost macabre, Toni thought, to be so happy in these surroundings, but she was, and, looking across at Rupert, she knew he was too.

They had just completed splinting the two legs together when there was a shout from outside and a powerful beam of light filled the doorway.

'Want any help?' asked a voice, and a policeman scrambled down the shifting mound from the broken doorway, then said, 'Strewth!' in an awed voice when he saw them both bending over the unconscious body of the gunman.

Everything happened very fast from then on. The police alerted an ambulance, and, because of the state of the ruins, the fire brigade.

Rupert and Antonia stayed with their patient, sitting on either side of him in a protective, proprietorial fashion. He was reasonably comfortable and warm, covered with a car rug. His face was still ghastly grey, but, swabbed by Toni with antiseptic wipes from Rupert's case, cleaner. She had also moistened his lips with sterile water when he had mumbled that he was thirsty.

With difficulty Rupert convinced the police that they wouldn't get any sense out of the gunman if they questioned him at that moment. The fire brigade and the ambulance men arrived at the same time, and together they worked out a strategy for widening the gap so that the casualty could be removed on a stretcher.

'We'll take over, Doctor,' offered the paramedic. 'You and the nurse must be all in after this little caper.'

'Thanks, that's an offer we can't refuse,' said Rupert, speaking for them both. He confirmed with the senior policeman that they could leave. Together they checked their patient once more and at last climbed out of the ruins into what had become a brilliant, moonlit night.

Oddly, once outside on the moon-washed hillside, Toni felt shy of Rupert.

'I'll follow you in the Mini,' she said as they reached the barbed-wire fence that had been cut to let the fire appliance and the ambulance through.

'No.' He laid a hand on her arm. 'Please don't. Come with me in the Range Rover. Antonia, indulge me in this. I don't think I can take any more tonight. The thought of you slipping and sliding in that little tin can down the hill is too terrifying.'

Toni drew herself up in the regal way that she had, reminding him of that first afternoon at the nursery. 'Do you mind?' she said. 'It's a Mini, and Granny gave it to me.'

He grinned down at her. 'OK, it's a well bred tin can, caviare, not sardines, but it's still got little wheels, and I don't want to let you out of my sight tonight, until we've got everything settled between us.'

'It's after eleven, and Grandpa will be worried sick about me.'

'Yes to the first, no to the second. I used the car phone.'

'I can't abandon my Mini.'

'Of course not. We'll switch off the ignition, radio and all the other paraphernalia, lock it up, and collect it tomorrow. It'll be safe as houses here tonight, with the police hovering around. Darling, I promise you all will be well.' Rupert took her hand, and they walked along the moonlit rutted track to the Mini.

Even Beethoven had to come to an end some time, she thought, as they approached and the thunderous chords of the Fifth Symphony failed to greet them, instead the gentler tones of Mozart's *Eine Kleine Nachtmusik* wafted over Windmill Hill.

It took only a minute or so to switch off the ignition and radio and retrieve the emergency lamp from the roof of the car, then they were on their way, back along the track to Rupert's Range Rover.

The journey down to Timbers took only a few minutes, but when they arrived at the entrance Rupert turned left towards the glasshouses, and not right to the house as Toni had expected.

He stopped, undid her seatbelt and helped her out. 'Is it locked?' he asked, indicating the potting-shed.

'Yes, but there's a spare key under the waterbutt at the corner.'

He found the key, unlocked the door, took her hand and led her into the soft, moonlit warmth of the potting-shed. He pulled an ancient wooden stool from beneath the bench.

'Sit here,' he said, softly, firmly. 'I'm going to comb your hair. It's what I wanted to do the first time I saw you—well, I wanted to touch it when you took off that ridiculous cap.' With capable fingers he released her tresses from the remains of the coronet that had been badly mauled by the barbed wire. 'Now, tell me what it is that you have to tell me before I may propose again.' His voice was as soft and gentle as his hands as they combed and coaxed her long silver-gold hair into some sort of order.

She wasn't afraid any more. She knew he would listen and understand, but it was still an effort to begin, to say the words. She took a deep breath.

'I was raped,' she said baldly. 'About a year ago, by a medical student at the hospital, Tim Dawson. Apparently he had a thing about me. One night as I was going back to the nurses' home in the rain, he jumped out at me from the bushes.' She shook her hair free from his fingers and hid her face in her hands. 'He raped me. He was like an animal.' Tears streamed down her cheeks. 'It hurt—really hurt, not just physically all over, but in my mind, in my heart.'

She breathed in hard, noisily. 'You see, it wasn't just what he did physically, but what he said about my fiancé, Patrick. Patrick and I had decided to wait for marriage, and everyone seemed to believe that I'd made life difficult for Patrick and he'd had to look elsewhere for sex. It wasn't like that, Rupert, honestly it wasn't. He said he didn't mind, and I. . .'

'You, my darling?' Rupert's voice was very strong and steady.

'Me? It didn't seem very important. I believed what he said about sex and all that only being a small part of life.'

'Well, so it is, my love, but it is important.' Rupert gathered her in his arms, but he knew she hadn't really noticed. 'And how do you feel about making love with me?' he asked, his words muffled as he whispered into her silver-gold hair.

'I want it more than anything in the world,' she said simply. 'I want you to love me. I want you to touch me. I love you touching me.'

'I'm glad about that,' he said drily, but for once his dry humour was lost on Toni.

She continued almost as if he hadn't spoken, 'I thought I hated Tim for what he'd done to me, but I didn't—I couldn't. It was awful feeling, thinking it was my fault, but not knowing why. Poor boy—he was only a boy really, it was the first time for him.'

'And for you, love, because of your understanding with *Patrick*.' Rupert spat the name out violently. 'It was the first time for you?'

'Yes.' She frowned, and Rupert smoothed the creases between her eyebrows with a gentle finger. 'I don't know why Patrick pretended not to mind about the sex business. I think perhaps he was kidding me.'

'I think, my darling, he probably was,' he agreed.

'But why?'

'I've no idea.' But he did. He was sure that the unspeakable bastard had played along with Antonia's natural reserve because he knew he was on to a good thing. A wealthy young woman from an impeccable background—what an asset for an ambitious young medical man with limited resources of his own.

'Rupert?' Toni queried.

'My darling?'

'You're not——' She hesitated and took hold of one of his hands tightly. 'You're not pretending, are you, not to mind about what happened to me? I couldn't bear that.'

'Of course I bloody well mind what happened to you, you dear silly girl, but if you mean am I pretending to love you out of some kind of outmoded chivalry, no, I damned well am not.' He caught her closer and kissed her hard. 'There, satisfied?'

'No, not really,' she said to tease him. Her tears had vanished; her grey eyes were bright with love and passion.

Rupert teased her back, pretending to be severe. 'Well, you'll have to contain yourself for a little longer, my dear. I want you to tell me all that happened that night and the aftermath—that must have been nearly as horrific as the rape itself, poor love.'

'Oh, Rupert, you really do understand. Are you sure you want to hear all the sordid details?'

'Positive. That way we'll neither of us have any hang-ups in the future, if life gets a bit difficult.' Toni made a little gesture of disbelief that such a thing could ever happen to them. He continued firmly, 'As might happen even in the long and unbelievably happy marriage that we're going to have.' Unrepentant, he smiled down at her. 'We will neither of us feel cheated.'

She looked at him now with solemn eyes. 'Rupert, you really are very wise.'

'Old and wise,' he said, kissing her again, this time gently. 'Now tell all, please.'

Hesitatingly, and at first reluctantly, she related the unpleasant details of the rape, and because he was quiet and attentive, she found the words coming more easily and she was able to look at him as she spoke.

'I did all the wrong things, of course, after Tim had left. I didn't see anybody on my way back to the nurses' home, so I bathed and showered—twice, actually,' she shuddered, remembering how dirty she had felt, 'and then went to bed. I just lay awake all night thinking about what had happened, thinking about Tim, even trying to find excuses for him.' She stared into space.

'When did you get around to reporting it?'

'Not for a couple of days. I had days off, you see, and came down here to Timbers as arranged. Of course, Granny spotted that something was wrong, but I couldn't tell her at once. When I did, she contacted Uncle Morris, both as her great friend and my GP. He was wonderful—so kind and understanding.'

'Good old Meredith,' muttered Rupert.

'He and Granny contacted the SNO at the hospital, and things started to happen. There was an enquiry, but because of the lapse of time, I was only half believed. Tim at first denied what had happened and then retracted, but he said I'd asked him to—to make love to me, because I'd said to get on with it, before he actually. . .' She hid her face against Rupert's chest. She went on in a muffled voice, 'I agreed when they asked me if I had said that, though I tried to explain that I was sort of playing for time, trying to reach the real Tim. But it was so ghastly sitting there being interrogated by so many people. I just wanted to get it over with.'

'Let me guess. He was believed—well, more or less, and you were advised not to take further action.'

'How did you know?' Toni turned a surprised face up to him.

Well, that's the way of the world, dear love. Admin people like everything clear-cut. Of course, you didn't help by not reporting what happened immediately, but the outcome might well have been the same whatever course you'd followed.' Rupert paused. 'And Patrick?'

'He had some leave due. He went away and wrote and said that he thought I'd prefer not to remain engaged after such a traumatic experience, but that I could keep his ring.' Rupert hugged her silently. 'He insulted me far more than poor Tim ever did. My counsellor—the hospital arranged for me to be counselled,' she explained with a twisted little smile, 'said I was suffering from a sort of double rape, and she was dead right, that's how I felt, humiliated on every front. And then Granny died, and that was worse than anything that had happened. I loved her very dearly.'

'I'm sure I would have loved her too, from all I've heard about her,' said Rupert softly.

'Oh, yes, you would, and she would have loved you in return. She was a remarkable person, you know.'

'I've no doubt about that. She seems to have managed the brigadier with extraordinary ease, and I should say he's no walkover.'

Toni giggled, and Rupert hid a pleased smile, knowing she was recovering something of her usual spirit. 'I do believe you're quite in awe of Grandpa,' she said.

'Isn't everyone?'

'I used to be, but I'm not any more. He's changed since Granny died. We've become quite close. He's softer, less rigid. He's never spoken to me, you know, about what happened at the hospital, or even about

Patrick and the broken engagement. I know Granny told him everything, but he gave no sign, just put an announcement in *The Times* that the engagement was off, and virtually ignored me. I sometimes wondered if even he thought it might have been my fault. But he's been sweet over the last few months, and we now have a terrific rapport with each other.'

Rupert smiled at her. 'I'm glad to hear it, my darling. Do you think he'll find me an acceptable grandson-in-law?'

'Oh, yes, he thinks you're the tops since you cured his ulcer. "A splendid young feller".' Toni tried to imitate the brigadier's military tones.

'It wasn't me,' said Rupert. 'That particular treatment pack was just made for his brand of ulcer, together with the nursing and TLC that went with it.'

Toni said with pretended horror, 'Don't ever tell him that. Let him think you worked a miracle.'

'If you say so, dear heart.'

'Oh, yes, I do.' He was holding her close, his face looking down at hers. 'Kiss me, Rupert,' she murmured.

'Like this,' he said, showering kisses on her face, 'and this.' His mouth travelled down her neck and into the V of her unbuttoned uniform dress and then back to her mouth. His arms crushed her to him and they stood for a long time, mouth to mouth, his hard body moulded to her soft, yielding one. His hands moved down her back and over her neat buttocks.

Toni gently pulled her face away from his, and looked up at him with her clear grey eyes. For one awful moment he thought he had frightened her off. 'What is it, love?' he asked softly.

Her eyes gleamed. 'You know, I don't know whether I should believe all this love stuff from you, Dr Devenish.'

Her voice told him she was teasing, but he contrived

to look apprehenisve and astonished. 'Dear God,' he said, raising his eyebrows, 'what have I done to bring this about?'

'I'd like to know why you showed definite signs, sir, of going off me a few days ago.' She put a finger to his lips. 'And don't deny it, my darling, because you did.'

He gave her one of his tenderest and most loving smiles. 'Yes I did, didn't I? You know, love, I really tried for about twenty-four hours to get you out of my system. You seemed more distant than ever. I suddenly wondered what I was doing pursuing a girl some fifteen years younger than me, who wouldn't even trust me with her deadly dark secret. I lost my nerve, thought it wasn't worth the effort.'

She looked at him in astonishment. 'Didn't you realise that I loved you?' she asked. 'I thought you knew everything—you always seemed totally self-sufficient.'

He looked horrified. 'Oh, my darling girl, don't think that. I'll be nothing on my own. I need you. Together we can do anything—at work, at play, we're a team.'

'You mean a matrimonial team?' she asked in a teasing voice. 'That is if you propose again and I accept.'

'What else, my darling, lovely girl, could be better than to emulate our partnership on the tennis court and make it a mixed double?'

'A winning mixed double?'

'Championship stuff all the way, give or take a few love games.'

'Oh, Rupert, I do love you.' She turned her face up to his. 'Kiss me, please—properly.'

He cupped her chin with one hand and stroked back her long silver-gold hair with the other. Slowly he trailed his lips across her forehead. 'Close your eyes,' he whispered, and, when she obligingly did so, he planted a butterfly kiss on each lid, and one on the tip of her nose. Then his firm lips were on her mouth, and very gently his tongue probed her lips apart and he explored her mouth, until with equal passion she responded.

They drew apart at last and Rupert smiled down at her, his fabulous gentian-blue eyes gleaming. 'Dear love,' he said, 'I hate to break this up, but it is almost the witching hour and we have work to do tomorrow.'

'And a match to win, had you forgotten?'

Rupert shook his head. 'Certainly not. I'm looking forward to every stroke with you by my side, partner.'

'Just like the rest of our life,' breathed Toni, as they stepped out into the moonlight and she carefully locked the potting-shed behind them.

'You'd better believe it,' drawled Rupert, 'as our poor friend up there would undoubtedly say.' He pointed up to Windmill Hill, visible now in the bright moonlight from the gravel sweep of drive where they had first met and fallen in love on that hot afternoon in May.

THE PERFECT GIFT FOR MOTHER'S DAY

Specially selected for you – four tender and heartwarming Romances written by popular authors.

LEGEND OF LOVE -
Melinda Cross

AN IMPERFECT AFFAIR -
Natalie Fox

LOVE IS THE KEY -
Mary Lyons

LOVE LIKE GOLD -
Valerie Parv

Available from February 1993   Price: £6.80

Mills & Boon

Discover the thrill of 4 Exciting Medical Romances – FREE

FREE

BOOKS FOR YOU

In the exciting world of modern
medicine, the emotions of true love
have an added drama. Now you can
experience four of these
unforgettable romantic tales of passion
and heartbreak FREE – and look forward to
a regular supply of Mills & Boon
Medical Romances delivered direct to your door!

❧ ❧ ❧

Turn the page for details of 2 extra
free gifts, and how to apply.

An Irresistible Offer from Mills & Boon

Here's an offer from Mills & Boon to become a regular reader of Medical Romances. To welcome you, we'd like you to have four books, a cuddly teddy and a special MYSTERY GIFT, all absolutely free and without obligation.

Then, every month you could look forward to receiving 4 more **brand new** Medical Romances for £1.70 each, delivered direct to your door, post and packing free. Plus our newsletter featuring author news, competitions, special offers, and lots more.

This invitation comes with no strings attached. You can cancel or suspend your subscription at any time, and still keep your free books and gifts.

Its so easy. Send no money now. Simply fill in the coupon below and post it at once to -

Mills & Boon Reader Service, FREEPOST, PO Box 236, Croydon, Surrey CR9 9EL

NO STAMP REQUIRED

YES! Please rush me my 4 Free Medical Romances and 2 Free Gifts! Please also reserve me a Reader Service Subscription. If I decide to subscribe, I can look forward to receiving 4 brand new Medical Romances every month for just £6.80, delivered direct to my door. Post and packing is free, and there's a free Mills & Boon Newsletter. If I choose not to subscribe I shall write to you within 10 days - I can keep the books and gifts whatever I decide. I can cancel or suspend my subscription at any time. I am over 18.

EP20D

Name (Mr/Mrs/Ms) _____

Address _____

_____

_____ Postcode _____

Signature _____